W9-BUN-713

The
EMPTY
HOUSE

The
EMPTY
HOUSE

ROSAMUNDE
PILCHER

ST. MARTIN'S PRESS

ISBN   0-440-20254-X

Chapter 1

IT WAS THREE O'CLOCK on a Monday afternoon in July, sunny and warm, the hay-scented air cooled by a sea breeze which blew in from the north. From the top of the hill, where the road wound up and over the shoulder of Carn Edvor, the land sloped down to distant cliffs; farmland, ribboned with yellow gorse, broken by outcrops of granite, and patchworked into dozens of small fields. Like a quilt, thought Virginia, and saw the pasture fields as scraps of green velvet, the greenish gold of new-cut hay as shining satin, the pinkish gold of standing corn as something soft and furry, to be stroked and touched.

It was very quiet. But when she closed her eyes the sounds of the summer afternoon obtruded, singling themselves out, one by one, for her attention. The humming of the wind, soft in her ears, stirred the bracken. A car climbed the long hill from Porthkerris, changed gear, came on up the road. From farther away came that pleasant summer-sound, the bee-murmur of combine harvesters. She opened her eyes and counted three, all minimized by distance to toy-size, scarlet and tiny as the models that Nicholas pushed around his nursery carpet.

The approaching car appeared over the crest of the hill, driven very slowly, its occupants, including the driver, staring from open windows at the marvellous view. Their faces were red with sunburn, spectacles glinted, arms bulged in sleeveless blouses, the car seemed packed with humanity. As it passed the lay-by where Virginia had left her own car, one of the women in the back looked up and saw her watching them from the hillside. For a startling second their eyes met, and then the car had gone, around the next corner and away to Land's End.

Virginia looked at her watch. A quarter past three. She sighed and stood up, dusted grass and bracken fronds from the seat of her white jeans, walked back down the hill to her car. The leather seat was griddle-hot with sunshine. She turned the car and started back towards Porthkerris, her mind filled with random images. Of Nicholas and Cara, incarcerated in the alien London nursery, taken to Kensington Gardens each day by Nanny; to the Zoo and the Costume Museum and suitable films by their grandmother. It would be hot in London, stuffy and airless. She wondered if they had cut Nicholas's hair. She wondered if she should buy him a model combine harvester and send it to him with some suitable, informative, maternal letter.

Today I saw three of these working in the fields at Lanyon, and I thought of you and thought you would like a model so that you could see how it worked.

A letter for Lady Keile to read approvingly aloud because Nicholas, every inch a male, saw no reason in puzzling out his mother's writing if his grandmother was ready and willing to read it aloud to him. She thought of the other letter, the one from her heart.

My darling child, without you and Cara I am without reason, aimless. I drive around in the car because I can think of nothing else to do, and the car takes me to places that I used to know, and I watch and wonder who it is who drives the monster combine, turning out the hay bales, square and strong as neatly tied parcels.

The old farmhouses with their great barns and outbuildings were strung along the five miles of coast like uncut stones on a rugged necklace, so that there was no telling where the fields of Penfolda finished and those of the next farm started. And so distant were the combines that it was impossible to guess at the identity of the men who drove them, or the tiny figures who walked behind, forking the bales into rough stooks to stand and dry in the midsummer sun.

She was not even sure that he still lived here, that he still farmed Penfolda, and yet could not imagine him existing anywhere else in the world. She let her mind's eye, like the lens of some great camera, zoom down on to the busy scene. The figures sprang into focus, huge and clear, and he was there, high at the wheel of the combine harvester, shirt sleeves rolled back from brown forearms, his hair tousled by the wind. And because there was danger in moving in so close, Virginia swiftly presented him with a wife, pictured her walking across the fields with a basket, flasks of tea, and perhaps a fruit cake to eat, and she wore a pink cotton dress and a blue apron and her long bare legs were brown.

Mrs. Eustace Philips. Mr. and Mrs. Eustace Philips of Penfolda.

The car nosed over the crest of the hill, and the bay and the white beaches and the distant headlands spread out before her, and far below, spilling down to around the blue goblet of the harbour, were the clustered houses and the Norman church tower of Porthkerris.

Wheal House, where the Lingards lived, and with whom Virginia was staying, lay on the far side of Porthkerris. If she had been a stranger, new to the district and visiting it for the first time, she would have followed the main road which led right down into the town and out the other side, and consequently become hopelessly ensnared in crawling traffic and hordes of aimless sightseers who spilled off the narrow pavements, or stood about at strategic corners, sucking ice-creams, choosing postcards and gazing in shop windows filled with brass piskies and pottery mermaids and other horrors considered suitable as souvenirs.

But, because she was not a stranger, Virginia turned off the road long before the houses started and took the narrow, high-hedged lane that wound up and over the hill which stood at the back of the town. It was the long way home, by no means a short cut, but eventually emerged out on the main road again, through a tunnel of wild rhododendrons and not fifty yards from the main entrance to Wheal House.

There was a white-barred gate and a rough drive that ran up between hedges of pink-flowered escallonia. The house was neo-Georgian, pleasingly proportioned, with a pedimented porch over the front door. The drive swept up between shaven green lawns and flower-beds heavy with the scent of wallflowers, and as Virginia parked the car in the shade of the house, there was a sharp cacophony of barking, and Dora, Alice Lingard's old spaniel, emerged from the open front door where she had been lying, for coolness, on the polished floor of the hall.

Virginia stopped to pat her and speak to her and then went indoors, taking off her sunglasses because after the bright day outside, the house seemed pitch dark.

Across the hall the garden doors stood open to the patio, which, facing south and trapping all the sun, was a favourite spot of Alice's in all but really wintry weather. Today, because of the heat, she had unrolled the split cane awnings, and the bright canvas chairs and the low tables, already set out with tea things, were narrowly striped by the shadow patterns which they cast.

On the table in the middle of the hall lay the afternoon's mail. Two letters for Virginia, both with London postmarks. She laid down her handbag and her glasses and picked them up. One from Lady Keile and one from . . . Cara. The italic letters, which she learned at school, were painfully formed, dearly familiar.

> *Mrs. A. Keile,*
> *c/o Mrs. Lingard,*
> *Wheal House,*
> *Porthkerris,*
> *Cornwall.*

No mistakes, no mis-spellings. Virginia wondered if she had managed by herself or whether Nanny had had to help. With the letters in her hand she went on across the hall and out to where her hostess sat, reclining gracefully on a long chair, with some sewing in her lap. She was making a cushion cover, stitching silk cord around the edge of the coral velvet square, and the colour lay in her lap like some huge fallen rose petal.

She looked up. "There you are! I was wondering what had happened to you. I thought perhaps you'd got stuck in a traffic jam."

Alice Lingard was a tall, dark woman in her late thirties, her firmly-built figure belied by long and slender arms and legs. She was what Virginia always thought of as a middle-aged friend, not middle-aged in the strictest sense of the word, but belonging to that generation which lay half-way between Virginia and Virginia's mother. She was, in fact, a lifelong family friend, and years ago had been a small bridesmaid at Virginia's mother's wedding.

She herself had married, eighteen years or so ago, Tom Lingard, then a young man on the verge of taking over the small family business of Lingard Sons which specialized in the manufacture of heavy engineering machinery in the nearby town of Fourbourne. Under Tom's chairmanship the firm had expanded and prospered, and after a series of successful take-over bids now controlled interests which spread from

Bristol to St. Just, and included mining rights, a small shipping business and the sale of agricultural machinery.

They had never had children, but Alice had diverted her natural domestic talents to her house and garden, and over the years had transformed what had once been a fairly unimaginative establishment into an enchanting house and a garden which was constantly being photographed and written about by the Garden Editors of the glossier magazines. Ten years ago, when Virginia and her mother had come to Cornwall to spend Easter with the Lingards, the work had only just started. This time, having not visited Wheal House during the intervening years, Virginia had scarcely recognized the place. Everything had been subtly altered, straight lines curved, outlines and boundaries magically removed. Trees had grown up, casting long shadows on smooth lawns which seemed to spread as far as the eye could see. The old orchard had been transformed to a wild garden tangled with all the sweetest of old-fashioned roses, and where once had drilled rows of runner beans and raspberry canes, now stood magnolias, creamy petalled, and heady-scented azaleas taller than a man could reach.

But, domestically, the patio was Alice's most successful project, neither house nor garden, but with the combined charm of both. Geraniums spilled from terrace pots, and up a trellised wall she had started to train a dark purple-flowered clematis. She had lately decided that she would also grow a vine, and was currently picking the brains of both friends and reference books, to decide on the best way to set about doing this. Her energies appeared to be endless.

Virginia pulled up a chair and dropped into it, surprised to find how hot and tired she felt. She shucked off her sandals and propped up her bare feet on to a handy stool. "I didn't go to Porthkerris."

"You didn't? But I thought you'd gone to the post office."

"I only wanted some stamps. I can buy them another time. There were so many people and so many buses and so much crushed and sweating humanity that I got claustrophobia and never stopped. Just went on driving."

"I can lend you stamps," said Alice. "Let me pour you some tea." She laid down her sewing and sat up to reach for the teapot. Steam rose from the delicate cup, fragrant, refreshing.

"Milk or lemon?"

"Lemon would be delicious."

"So much more refreshing, I think, on a hot day." She handed Virginia the cup and lay back again. "Where did you drive?"

"Um? . . . oh, the other way . . ."

"Land's End?"

"Not so far. I only got as far as Lanyon. I parked the car in a lay-by and climbed the hill for a bit and sat in the bracken and looked at the view."

"So beautiful," said Alice, threading her needle.

"They're cutting hay on the farms."

"Yes, they would be."

"It never changes, does it? Lanyon, I mean. No new houses, no new roads, no shops, no caravan parks." She took a mouthful of scalding hot lapsang suchong and then, with care, laid the cup and saucer down on the paved floor beside her chair. "Alice, does Eustace Philips still farm Penfolda?"

Alice stopped sewing, and put up a hand to take off her dark glasses and stare at Virginia. There was a puzzled frown between her dark brows.

"What do you know about Eustace Philips? How do you know him?"

"Alice, your memory is appalling. It was you yourself who took me out there, you and Tom, for an enormous barbecue on the cliffs at Penfolda. There must have been at least thirty people and I don't know who organized it, but we cooked sausages over a fire and drank beer out of a barrel. Oh, surely you remember, and then Mrs. Philips gave us tea in her kitchen!"

"Now you remind me, of course I do. It was bitterly cold but quite beautiful and we watched the moon rise from behind Boscovey Head. I do remember. Now, who was it who threw that party? It certainly wasn't Eustace, he was always too busy milking cows. It must have been the Barnets—he was a sculptor and had a studio for a couple of years in Porthkerris before he went back to London. His wife wove baskets or belts or something, terribly folksy, and they had a lot of children who never wore shoes. They were always thinking up the most original parties. It must have been the Barnets . . . How extraordinary! I hadn't thought about them in years. And we all went out to Penfolda." But here her memory let her down. She looked at Virginia blankly. "Or did we? Who went to that party?"

"Mother didn't come. She said it wasn't up her street . . ."

"How right she was."

"But you and I and Tom went."

"Of course. Bundled up in sweaters and socks. I'm not sure I didn't wear a fur coat. But we were talking about Eustace. How old were you, Virginia? Seventeen? Fancy your remembering Eustace Philips after all these years."

"You haven't answered my question. Is he still at Penfolda?"

"As the farm belonged to his father, and *his* father, and as far as I know *his* father before that, do you really think it likely that Eustace would up sticks and depart?"

"I suppose not. It's just that they were cutting hay this afternoon and I wondered if it was he who drove one of the combines. Do you ever see him, Alice?"

"Hardly ever. Not because we don't want to, understand me, but he's a hard-working farmer, and Tom's so busy being a tycoon, that their paths don't often cross. Except sometimes they meet at the hare shoot, or the Boxing Day meet . . . you know the sort of thing."

Virginia picked up her tea-cup and saucer, and observed, minutely, the rose painted upon its side.

"He's married," she said.

"You say that as though you were stating an irrefutable fact."

"Aren't I?"

"No, you're not. He never married. Heaven knows why. I always thought he was so attractive in a sun-burned, D. H. Lawrence-ish sort of way. There must have been a number of languishing ladies in Lanyon, but he resisted the lot. He must like it that way."

Eustace's wife, so swiftly imagined, as swiftly died, a wraith blown to nothing by the cold wind of reality. Instead, Virginia saw the Penfolda kitchen, cheerless and untidy, with the remains of the last meal abandoned on the table, dishes in the sink, an ashtray filled with cigarette stubs.

"Who looks after him?"

"I don't know. His mother died a couple of years ago I believe . . . I don't know what he does. Perhaps he's got a sexy housekeeper, or a domesticated mistress? I really don't know."

And couldn't care less, her tone implied. She had finished sewing on the silk cord, now gave a couple of neat firm stitches and then broke the thread with a little tug. "There, that's done. Isn't it a divine colour? But it's really too hot to sew." She laid it aside. "Oh dear, I suppose I must go and see what we'll have for dinner. What would you say to a delicious fresh lobster?"

"I'd say 'pleased to see you.' "

Alice stood up, unfolding her long height to tower over Virginia. "Did you see your letters?"

"Yes, they're here."

Alice stooped to pick up the tray. "I'll leave you," she said, "to read them in peace."

Keeping the best to the last, Virginia opened her mother-in-law's letter first. The envelope was dark blue, lined with navy blue tissue. The writing-paper was thick, the address blackly embossed at its head.

32 Welton Gardens, S.W.8.

My dear Virginia,

I hope you are enjoying this wonderful weather, quite a heatwave and into the nineties yesterday. I expect you are swimming in Alice's pool, such a joy not having to drive to the beach every time you want to swim.

The children are both well and send their love. Nanny takes them into the park every day and they take their tea with them and eat it there. I took Cara to Harrods this morning to buy some new dresses, she is getting so tall and was quite out of her old ones. One is blue with appliquéd flowers, the other pink with a little smocking. I think you would approve!

Tomorrow they are going to tea with the Manning-Prestons. Nanny is looking forward to a good gossip with their Nanny, and Susan is just the right age for Cara. It would be nice for them to be friends.

My regards to Alice, and let me know when you decide to come back to London, but we are managing beautifully, and don't want you to cut short your holiday at all for any reason. You really were due for one.

Affectionately,
Dorothea Keile

She read the letter twice, torn by conflicting emotions. Double meanings sprang at her from between the meticulously-penned, well-turned sentences. She saw her children in the park, the baked London grass turned yellow in the heat, trodden and tired, and fouled by dogs. She saw the white-hot morning sky high above the roof tops and the little girl being fitted into dresses that she would neither like nor want, but would be too polite to reject. She saw the Manning-Prestons's tall, terraced house, with the paved garden at the back where Mrs. Manning-Preston held her famous cocktail parties, and where Cara and Susan would be sent to play while the Nannies talked about knitting patterns and what a terror Nanny Brigg's little charge was going to be. And she saw Cara standing silent, petrified with shyness, and Susan Manning-Preston treating her with contempt because Cara wore spectacles and Susan thought she was a ninny.

And "we are managing beautifully." The statement seemed to Virginia completely ambiguous. Who was "we"? Nanny and the grandmother? Or did it include the children, Virginia's children? Did they let Cara sleep with the old Teddy that Nanny swore was unhygienic? Did they remember always to leave the light on so that Nicholas could get himself to the bathroom in the middle of the night? And were they ever left alone, disorganized, dirty, untidy, to play secret, pointless games in small corners of the garden, with perhaps a nut or a leaf, and all the imaginings that were contained within their small, clever, bewildering brains?

She found that her hands were shaking. She was a fool to get into this state. Nanny had looked after the children since they were born, she knew all their idiosyncrasies and nobody could cope with Nicholas's sudden rages better than she.

(But should he have such rages? At six, shouldn't he have grown out of them? What frustration sparks them off?)

And Nanny was gentle with Cara. She made dolls' clothes and knitted scarves and sweaters for the teddies out of left-over bits of wool. And she let Cara wheel her doll's perambulator into the park; over the crossing by the Albert Memorial, they went. (But did she read to Cara, the books that Cara loved? *The Borrowers* and *The Railway Children* and every word of *The Secret Garden*.) Did she love the children, or simply possess them?

These were all familiar questions which, lately, had been raising themselves with ever-increasing frequency within the confines of Virginia's own head. But never answered. Knowing that she was evading a vital issue, she would shelve her own anxiety, always with some excuse to herself. I can't think about it now, I'm too tired. Perhaps in a couple of years when Nicholas goes away to Prep. school, perhaps then I'll tell my mother-in-law that I don't need Nanny any longer; I'll say to Nanny it's time to go, to find another new baby to look after. And perhaps just now I'm too emotional, I wouldn't be good for the children; they're better with Nanny: after all, she's been looking after children for forty years.

Like a familiar sedative the well-worn excuses came pat, blunting Virginia's uneasy conscience. She put the blue letter back into its expensive envelope and turned, in relief, to the second one. But the relief was short-lived. Cara had borrowed her grandmother's writing-paper, but the sentences this time were neither meticulously penned nor well-turned. The ink was blotched and the lines ran down the side of the paper as though the words were tumbling hopelessly downhill.

> *Darling Mother,*
> *I hope you are having a good time. I hope it is nise wether. It is hot in London. I have to go and have tea with Susan Maning Preston. I dont no what we will play. Last night Nicholas screemed and Granny had to give him a pil. He went all red. One of my dolls eyes has come out and I cant find it. Please will you rite to me soon and tell me when we are going back to Kirkton.*
> *With love from Cara.*
> *P.S. Dont forget to rite.*

She folded the letter and put it away. Across the garden, across the lawns, the blue of Alice's swimming-pool glimmered like a jewel. The cooling air was filled with bird-song and the scent of flowers. From inside the house she could hear Alice's voice talking to Mrs. Jilkes, the cook, doubtless about the lobster which they were going to eat for dinner.

She felt helpless, totally inadequate. She thought of asking Alice to have the children here, and in the next instant knew that it was impossible. Alice's house was not designed for children, her life did not cater for their inclusion. She would be irritated beyond words by Cara forgetting to change her gum-boots, or by Nicholas kicking his football into the treasured flower-borders, or drawing "pictures" on the wallpaper. For without Nanny, he would doubtless be impossible because he was always twice as naughty without her to keep an eye on him.

Without Nanny. Those were the operative words. On her own. She had to have them on her own.

And yet the very thought filled her with dread. What would she do with them? Where would they go? Like feelers her thoughts probed around, searching for ideas. A hotel? But hotels here would be filled to the brim with summer visitors and terribly expensive. Besides, Nicholas in a hotel would be as nerve-racking as Nicholas at Wheal House. She thought of hiring a caravan, or camping with them on the beach, like the summer migration of hippies, who lit fires of driftwood and slept curled up on the chilly sand.

Of course, there was always Kirkton. Some time, she would have to go back. But all her instincts shied away from the thought of returning to Scotland, to the house where she had lived with Anthony, the place where her children had been born, the only place they thought of as home. Thinking of Kirkton, she saw tree shadows flickering on pale walls, the cold northern light reflected on the white ceilings, the sound of her own feet going up the uncarpeted, polished stairway. She thought of clear autumn evenings when the first skeins of geese flew over, and the park, in front of the house, sweeping down to the banks of the deep, swift-flowing river . . .

No. Not yet. Cara would have to wait. Later, perhaps, they would go back to Kirkton. Not yet. Behind her a door slammed, and she was jerked back to reality by the arrival of Tom Lingard, back from work. She heard him call Alice, then drop his brief-case on the hall-table, and come out to the patio in search of his wife.

"Hallo, Virginia." He bent and dropped a kiss on the top of her head. "All alone? Where's Alice?"

"Interviewing a lobster in the kitchen."

"Letters from the children? All well? Well done, that's great . . ." One of Tom's idiosyncrasies was that he never bothered to wait for an answer to any of his questions. Virginia sometimes wondered if this was the secret of his outstanding success. "What have you been doing all day? Lying in the sun? That's the job. How about coming and having a swim with me now? The exercise'll do you good after all this lazing about. We'll get Alice to come too . . ." He went, spring-footed and bursting with energy, back into the house and down the passage towards the kitchen, bellowing for his wife. And Virginia, grateful for directions, stood up and collected her mail and went indoors, obediently, and upstairs to her bedroom to change into a bikini.

Chapter 2

THE SOLICITORS WERE called Smart, Chirgwin and Williams. At least, those were the names on the brass plate by the door, a plate which had been polished so long and so hard that the letters had lost their sharpness and were quite difficult to read. There was a brass knocker on the door, too, and a brass door knob, as smooth and shining as the plate, and when Virginia turned the knob and opened the door, she stepped into a narrow hall of polished brown linoleum and shining cream paint and it occurred to her that some hard-working woman was using up an awful lot of elbow grease.

There was a glass window, like an old-fashioned ticket-office with INQUIRIES written over it, and a bell to press. Virginia pressed the bell and the window flew up.

"Yes?"

Startled, Virginia told the face behind the window that she wanted to see Mr. Williams.

"Have you got an appointment?"

"Yes. It's Mrs. Keile."

"Just a moment, please."

The window slammed down and the face withdrew. Presently a door opened and the face reappeared, along with a well-upholstered body and a pair of legs that went straight down into sturdy lace-up shoes.

"If you'd like to come this way, Mrs. Keile."

The building which housed the solicitors' office stood at the top of the hill which led out of Porthkerris, but even so Virginia was taken unawares by the marvellous view which leapt at her as soon as she walked into the room. Mr. Williams's desk stood in the middle of the carpet and Mr. Williams was, even now, getting to his feet behind it. But, beyond Mr. Williams, a great picture-window framed, like some lovely painting, the whole jumbled, charming panorama of the old part of the town. Roofs of houses, faded slate and whitewashed chimneys, tumbled without pattern or order down the hill. Here a blue door, there a yellow window; here a window-sill bright with geraniums, a line of washing gay as flags, or the leaves of some unsuspected and normally unseen tree. Beyond the roofs and far below them was the harbour, at full tide and sparkling with sunshine. Boats rocked at anchor and a white sail sped out beyond the shelter of the harbour wall, heading for the ruler line of the horizon where the two blues met. The air was clamorous with the sound of gulls, the sky patterned with their great gliding wings and as Virginia stood there, the church bells from the Norman tower struck up a simple carillon and clock chimes rang out eleven o'clock.

"Good morning," said Mr. Williams, and Virginia realized that he had already said this twice. She tore her attention from the view and tried to focus it on him.

"Oh, good morning. I'm Mrs. Keile, I . . ." But it was impossible. "How *can* you work in a room with a view like that?"

"That's why I sit with my back to it . . ."

"It's breathtaking."

"Yes, and quite unique. We're often asked by artists if they can paint the harbour from this window. You can see the whole structure of the town, and the colours are always different, always beautiful. Except, of course, on a rainy day. Now—" his manner changed abruptly as though anxious to get down to work and to waste no more time— "what can I do for you?" He drew a chair forward for her.

Trying to stop looking out of the window and to concentrate on the matter in hand, Virginia sat down. "Well I've maybe come to quite the wrong person, but you see I can't find an estate agent anywhere in the town. And I looked in the local paper for a house to rent, but there didn't seem to be one. And then I saw your name in the telephone book, and I thought perhaps you might be able to help me."

"Help you find a house?" Mr. Williams was young, very dark, his eyes frankly interested in the attractive woman who faced him across his desk.

"Just to rent . . ."

"For how long?"

"A month . . . my children go back to school the first week in September."

"I see. Well, we don't actually *deal* in this sort of thing, but I could ask Miss Leddra if there's anything that she could suggest. But of course this is the high season, and the town is already packed to the gunwales with visitors. Even if you do find something, I'm afraid you'll have to pay a fairly steep rent."

"I don't mind."

"Well, just a moment . . ."

He left her and went out, and Virginia heard him speaking to the woman who had let her in. She got up and went back to the window, and opened it wide and laughed as a furious gull flew crossly off the sill where he had been perching. The wind off the sea was cool and fresh. A pleasure boat packed with passengers started off across the harbour and suddenly Virginia longed to be on board, irresponsible, sunburned, wearing a hat with KISS ME written on it and screaming with laughter as the first waves sent the boat rocking.

Mr. Williams came back. "Can you wait a moment? Miss Leddra's making a few inquiries . . ."

"Yes, of course." She returned to her chair.

"Are you staying in Porthkerris?" Mr. Williams asked conversationally.

"Yes. I'm staying with friends. The Lingards up at Wheal House."

His previous manner had been neither off-hand nor familiar, but all at once he was almost deferential.

"Oh yes, of course. What a charming place that is."

"Yes. Alice has made it lovely."

"Have you been there before?"

"Yes. Ten years ago. But I haven't been since."

"Are your children with you?"

"No. They're in London, with their grandmother. But I want to get them down here with me, if I can."

"Is London your home?"

"No. It's just that my mother-in-law lives in London." Mr. Williams waited. "My home . . . that is, we live in Scotland."

He looked delighted . . . Virginia could not think why it should delight him that she lived in Scotland. "But how splendid! What part?"

"In Perthshire."

"The most beautiful. My wife and I spent a holiday there last summer. The peace of it all, and the empty roads and the quiet. How could you bear to come away?"

Virginia had opened her mouth to tell him when the discussion was mercifully interrupted by the arrival of Miss Leddra, bearing a sheaf of papers.

"Here it is, Mr. Williams. Bosithick. And the letter from Mr. Kernow saying that if we could find a tenant for August he'd be willing to rent. But only to a *suitable* tenant, Mr. Williams. He's very firm about that point."

Mr. Williams took the papers and smiled at Virginia over the top of them.

"Are you a suitable tenant, Mrs. Keile?"

"It depends. On what you're offering me, doesn't it?"

"Well, it's not actually in Porthkerris . . . thank you, Miss Leddra . . . but not too far away . . . out at Lanyon actually . . ."

"Lanyon!"

She must have sounded appalled, for Mr. Williams sprang at once to Lanyon's defence. "But it's a most charming spot, quite the most beautiful bit of coastline left anywhere."

"I didn't mean that I didn't like it. I was just surprised."

"Were you? Why?"

He was too sharp, like a beady-eyed bird. "No reason, really. Tell me about the house."

He told her. It was an old cottage, neither distinguished nor beautiful, but with a small claim to fame in that a famous writer had once lived and worked there during the nineteen-twenties.

Virginia said, "Which?"

"I beg your pardon?"

"Which famous writer?"

"Oh, I'm sorry. Aubrey Crane. Didn't you know that he spent some years in this part of the world?"

Virginia did not. But Aubrey Crane had been one of the many authors of whom Virginia's mother did not approve. She remembered her mother's chill expression, lips pursed, whenever his books were mentioned; remembered them being returned swiftly to the library before the young Virginia could get her eyes on them. For some reason this seemed to make the cottage called Bosithick even more desirable. "Go on," said Virginia.

Mr. Williams went on. Despite its age Bosithick had been modernized to a certain degree—there was now a bathroom and a lavatory and an electric cooker.

"Who does it belong to?" Virginia asked.

"Mr. Kernow is the nephew of the old lady who used to own the house. She left it to him, but he lives in Plymouth so he uses it just for holidays. He and his family intended coming down for the summer, but his wife fell ill and can't make the trip. As we are Mr. Kernow's solicitors, he put the matter in our hands, with the instructions that, if we did let the house, it must be to a tenant who can be trusted to take care of it."

"How big is it?"

Mr. Williams perused his papers. "Let's see, a kitchen, a sitting-room, a downstairs bathroom, and a hall, and three rooms upstairs."

"Is there a garden?"

"Not really."

"How far is it from the road?"

"About a hundred yards down a farm lane as far as I can remember."

"And could I have it right away?"

"I can see no objection. But you must see it first."

"Yes, of course . . . when can I see it?"

"Today? Tomorrow?"

"Tomorrow morning."

"I'll take you out myself."

"Thank you, Mr. Williams." Virginia stood up and made for the door, and he had to make a little rush to get there and open it before she did.

"There's just one thing, Mrs. Keile."

"What's that?"

"You haven't asked what the rent is."

She smiled. "No I haven't, have I? Goodbye, Mr. Williams."

Virginia said nothing to Alice and Tom. She did not want to have to put into words what was, at best, only a vague idea. She did not want to be drawn into an argument, to be persuaded either that the children were best left in London with their grandmother or that Alice could disregard the possible destruction that they might perpetrate at Wheal House and would insist on having them there. When Virginia had found somewhere for them all to live, she would present Alice with what she had done as a *fait accompli*. And then Alice would maybe help her take the biggest hurdle of all, which was to persuade the grandmother to let the children come to Cornwall without Nanny. At the very prospect of this ordeal, Virginia's imagination turned and ran, but there were other and smaller obstacles to be overcome first, and these she was determined to do by herself.

Alice was a perfect hostess. When Virginia told her that she would be out for the morning it never occurred to Alice to quiz her as to what she intended doing. She only said, "Will you be in for lunch?"

"I don't think so . . . Better say not . . ."

"I'll see you at tea time, then. We'll have a swim together afterwards."

"Heaven," said Virginia. She kissed Alice and went out, got into her car and drove down the hill into Porthkerris. She parked the car near the station and walked to the solicitors' office to pick up Mr. Williams.

"Mrs. Keile, I couldn't be more sorry, but I'm not going to be able to come out with you this morning to Bosithick. An old client is coming down from Truro and I must be here to see her; I do hope you understand! But here are the keys of the house, and I've drawn a fairly detailed map of how to find it . . . I don't think you could go wrong. Do you mind going on your own, or would you like to take Miss Leddra with you?"

Virginia imagined the daunting presence of the formidable Miss Leddra and assured Mr. Williams that she'd manage perfectly on her own. She was given a ring of large keys, each with a wooden label. Front Door, Coal Shed, Tower Room. "You'll need to watch out for the lane," Mr. Williams told her, as they went together towards the door. "It's fairly bumpy and although there's no room to turn by the gate of Bosithick itself, you can manage easily if you carry on down the lane; you'll come to an old farmyard and you can turn the car there. Now, you're sure you'll be all right . . . I couldn't be more sorry about this, but I'll be here, of course, waiting to hear what you think of the place. Oh, and Mrs. Keile . . . it's been empty for some months. Try not to be influenced if it feels a little dingy. Just throw open a few windows and imagine it with a nice cheerful fire."

Slightly discouraged by these parting remarks, Virginia went back to her car. The keys of the unknown house weighed heavy as lead in her handbag. All at once, she longed for company, and even considered, for a mad moment, returning to Wheal House to make a true confession to Alice and persuade her to come out to Lanyon and lend a little moral support. But that was ridiculous. It was just a little cottage, to be viewed, and either rented or rejected. Any fool . . . even Virginia . . . could surely do that.

The weather was still beautiful and the traffic still appalling. She crawled, one of the long queue of cars, down into the depths of town and out the other side. At the top of the hill where the roads forked, the traffic thinned a little and she was able to put on some speed and pass a line of dawdling cars. As she went up and over the moor and the sea dropped and spread beneath her, her spirits rose. The road wound like a grey ribbon through the bracken-covered hillside; to her left towered the great outcrop of Carn Edvor stained purple with heather, and on her right the country swept away down to the sea, the familiar patchwork of fields and farms, that she had sat and watched only two days before.

She had been told by Mr. Williams to look out for a clump of wind-leaning hawthorns by the side of the road. Beyond this was a steep corner and then the narrow farm track which led down towards the sea. Virginia came upon it and turned the car down into it, no more than a stony lane high-hedged with brambles. She went into bottom gear and edged cautiously downhill, attempting to avoid bumps and pot-holes and trying not to think about the damage that the prickly gorse bushes were inflicting on the paintwork of her car.

There was no sign of any house, until she turned a steep corner and was instantly upon it. A stone wall, and beyond, a gable and a slated roof. She stopped the car in the lane, reached for her handbag and got out. There was a cool, salty wind blowing in from the sea, and the smell of gorse. She went to open the gate, but the hinges were broken and it had to be lifted before she could edge through. A path of sorts led down towards a flight of stone steps and so to the house, and Virginia saw that it was long and low with gables to the north and the south, and at the north end, looking out over the sea, had been added an extra room with a square tower above it. The tower imparted an oddly sanctified look to the house which Virginia found chilling. There was no garden to speak of, but at the south end a patch of unmown grass blew in the wind and two leaning poles supported what had once been a washing line.

She went down the steps and along a dank pathway that led along the side of the house towards the front door. This had once been painted dark red and was scarred with splitting sun blisters. Virginia took out the key and put it in the keyhole and turned the door knob and the key together and the door instantly, silently, swung inwards. She saw a tiny flight of stairs, a worn rung on bare boards, smelt damp and . . . mice? She swallowed nervously. She hated mice, but now that she had come so far there was nothing for it but to go up the two worn steps and tread gingerly over the threshold.

It did not take long to go over the old part of the house, to glance in at the tiny kitchen with its inadequate cooker and stained sink; the sitting-room cluttered with ill-matching chairs. An electric fire sat in the cavern of the huge old fireplace, like a savage animal at the mouth of its lair. There were curtains of flimsy cotton hanging at the windows, fly-blown and dejected, and a dresser packed with cups and plates and dishes in every sort of size and shape and state of dilapidation.

Without hope, Virginia went upstairs. The bedrooms were dim with tiny windows and unsuitable, looming pieces of furniture. She returned to the top of the stairs, and so up another pair of steps, to a closed door. She opened this, and after the gloom of the rest of the house, the blast of bright, northern light by which she was immediately assailed, was dazzling. Stunned by it, she stepped blindly into an astonishing room, small, completely square, windowed on three walls, it stood high above the sea like the bridge of a ship, with a view of the coastline that must have extended for fifteen miles.

A window-seat with a faded cover ran along the north side of this room. There was a scrubbed table, and an old braided rug and in the centre of the floor, like a decorative well-head, the wrought-iron banister of a spiral staircase which led directly down to the room beneath, the "Hall" of Mr. Williams's prospectus.

Cautiously Virginia descended, to a room dominated by an enormous *art nouveau* fireplace. Off this was the bathroom; and then another door, and she was back where she'd started, in the dark and depressing sitting-room.

It was an extraordinary, a terrible house. It sat around her, waiting for her to make some decision, contemptuous of her faintness of heart. To give herself time, she went back up to the tower room, sat on the window-seat and opened her bag to find a cigarette. Her last. She would have to buy some more. She lit it and looked at the bare scrubbed table, and the faded colours of the rug on the floor, and knew that this had been Aubrey Crane's study, the workroom where he had wrestled out the lusty love stories that Virginia had never been encouraged to read. She saw him, bearded and knickerbockered, his conventional appearance belying the passions of his rebellious heart. Perhaps in summertime, he would have flung wide these windows, to catch all the scents and sounds of the countryside, the roar of the sea, the whistle of the wind. But in winter it would be bitterly cold, and he would have to wrap himself in blankets, and write painfully with chilblained fingers mittened in knitted wool . . .

Somewhere in the room a fly droned, blundering against the window-pane. Virginia leaned her forehead on the cool glass of the window and stared sightless at the view and started one of the interminable ding-dong arguments she had been having with herself for years.

I can't come here.

Why not?

I hate it. It's spooky and frightening. It's got a horrible atmosphere.

That's just your imagination.

It's an impossible house. I could never bring the children here. They've never lived in such a place. Anyway, there's nowhere for them to play.

There's the whole world for them to play in. The fields and the cliffs and the sea.

But looking after them . . . the washing and the ironing, and the cooking. And there's no refrigerator, and how would I heat the water?

I thought that all that mattered was getting the children to yourself, away from London.

They're better in London, with Nanny, than living in a house like this.

That wasn't what you thought yesterday.

I can't bring them here. I wouldn't know where to begin. Not on my own like that.

Then what are you going to do?

I don't know. Talk to Alice, perhaps I should have talked to her before now. She hasn't children of her own, but she'll understand. Maybe she'll know about some other little house. She'll understand. She'll help. She has to help.

So much, said her own cool and scathing voice, *for all those strong resolutions*.

Angrily, Virginia stubbed out the half-smoked cigarette, ground it under her heel and got up and went downstairs and took out the keys and locked the door behind her. She went back up the path to the gate, stepped through and shut it. The house watched her the small bedroom windows like derisive eyes. She tore herself from their gaze and got back into the safety of her car. It was a quarter past twelve. She needed cigarettes and she was not expected back at Wheal House for lunch, so, when she had turned the car, and was driving back up on to the main road again, she took not the road to Porthkerris, but the other way, and she drove the short mile to Lanyon village, up the narrow main street, and finally came to a halt in the cobbled square that was flanked on one side by the porch of the square-towered church and on the other by a small whitewashed pub called The Mermaid's Arms.

Because of the fine weather, there were tables and chairs set up outside the pub, along with brightly coloured sun-umbrellas and tubs of orange nasturtiums. A man and a woman in holiday clothes sat and drank their beer, their little boy played with a puppy. As Virginia approached, they looked up to smile good morning, and she smiled back and went past them in through the door, instinctively ducking her head beneath the blackened lintel.

Inside it was dark-panelled, low-ceilinged, dimly illuminated by tiny windows veiled in lace curtains; there was a pleasant smell, cool and musty. A few figures, scarcely visible in the gloom, sat along the wall, or around small wobbly tables, and behind the bar, framed by rows of hanging beer-mugs, the barman, in shirtsleeves and a checkered pullover, was polishing glasses with a dishcloth.

". . . I don't know 'ow it is, William," he was saying to a customer who sat at the other end of the bar, perched disconsolately on a tall stool, with a long cigarette ash and half a pint of bitter, ". . . but you put the litter bins up and nobody puts nothing into them . . ."

"Ur . . ." said William, nodding in sad agreement and sprinkling cigarette ash into the beer.

"Stuff blows all over the road, and the County Council don't even come and empty them. Ugly old things they are, too, we'd be better without them. Managed all right without them before, we did . . ."

He finished polishing the glass, set it down with a thump and turned to attend to Virginia.

"Yes, madam?"

He was very Cornish, in voice, in looks, in colouring. A red and wind-burned face, blue eyes, black hair.

Virginia asked for cigarettes.

"Only got packets of twenty. That all right?" He turned to take them from the shelf and slit the wrapper with a practised thumb-nail. "Lovely day, isn't it? On holiday, are you?"

"Yes." It was years since she had been into a pub. In Scotland women were never taken into pubs. She had forgotten the atmosphere, the snug companionship. She said, "Do you have any Coke?"

He looked surprised. "Yes, I've got Coke. Keep it for the children. Want some, do you?"

"Please."

He reached for a bottle, opened it neatly, poured it into a glass and pushed it across the counter towards her.

"I was just saying to William, here, that road to Porthkerris is a disgrace . . ." Virginia pulled up a stool and settled down to listen. ". . . All that rubbish lying around. Visitors don't seem to know what to do with their litter. You'd think coming to a lovely part like this they'd have the sense they was born with and take all them old bits of paper home with them, in the car, not leave them lying around on the roadside. They talk about conservation and ecology, but, my God . . ."

He was off on what was obviously his favourite hobby-horse, judging by the well-timed grunts of assent that came from all corners of the room. Virginia lit a cigarette. Outside, in the sunny square, a car drew up, the engine stopped, a door slammed. She heard a man's voice say good morning, and then footsteps came through the doorway and into the bar behind her.

". . . I wrote to the MP about it, said who was going to get the place cleaned up, he said it was the responsibility of the County Council, but I said . . ." Over Virginia's head he caught sight of the new customer. " 'Allo, there! You're a stranger."

"Still at the litter bins, Joe?"

"You know me, boy, worry a subject to death, like a terrier killing a rat. What'll you have?"

"A pint of bitter."

Joe turned to draw the beer, and the newcomer moved in to stand between Virginia and lugubrious William, and she had recognized his voice at once, as soon as he spoke, just as she had known his footfall, stepping in over the flagged threshold of The Mermaid's Arms.

She took a mouthful of Coke, laid down the glass. All at once her cigarette tasted bitter; she stubbed it out and turned her head to look at him, and she saw the blue shirt, with the sleeves rolled back from his brown forearms, and the eyes very blue and the short, rough, brown hair cut like a pelt, close to the shape of his head. And because there was nothing else to be done she said, "Hallo, Eustace."

Startled, his head swung round and his expression was that of a man who had suddenly been hit in the stomach, bemused and incapable. She said, quickly, "It really is me," and his smile came, incredulous, rueful, as though he knew he had been made to look a fool.

"Virginia."

She said again, stupidly, "Hallo."

"What in the name of heaven are you doing here?"

She was aware that every ear in the place was waiting for her to reply. She made it very light and casual. "Buying cigarettes. Having a drink."

"I didn't mean that. I mean in Cornwall. Here, in Lanyon."

"I'm on holiday. Staying with the Lingards in Porthkerris."

"How long have you been here?"

"About a week . . ."

"And what are you doing out here?"

But before she had time to tell him, the barman had pushed Eustace's tankard of beer across the counter, and Eustace was diverted by trying to find the right money in his trouser pocket.

"Old friends, are you?" asked Joe, looking at Virginia with new interest, and she said, "Yes, I suppose you could say that."

"I haven't seen her for ten years," Eustace told him, pushing the coins across the counter. He looked at Virginia's glass. "What are you drinking?"

"Coke."

"Bring it outside, we may as well sit in the sun."

She followed him, aware of the unblinking stares which followed them; the insatiable curiosity. Outside in the sunshine he put their glasses down on to a wooden table and they settled, side by side on a bench, with the sun on their heads and their backs against the white-washed wall of the pub.

"You don't mind being brought out here, do you? Otherwise we couldn't say a word without it being received and transmitted all over the county within half an hour."

"I'd rather be outside."

Half turned towards her, he sat so close that Virginia could see the rough, weather-beaten texture of his skin, the network of tiny lines around his eyes, the first frosting of white in that thick brown hair. She thought, *I'm with him again.*

He said, "Tell me."

"Tell you what?"

"What happened to you." And then quickly: "I know you got married."

"Yes. Almost at once."

"Well, that would have put paid to the London Season you were dreading so much."

"Yes, it did."

"And the coming-out dance."

"I had a wedding instead."

"Mrs. Anthony Keile. I saw the announcement in the paper." Virginia said nothing. "Where do you live now?"

"In Scotland. There's a house in Scotland . . ."

"And children?"

"Yes. Two. A boy and a girl."

"How old are they?" He was really interested, and she remembered how the Cornish loved children, how Mrs. Jilkes was for ever going dewy-eyed over some lovely little great-nephew or niece.

"The girl's eight and the boy's six."

"Are they with you now?"

"No. They're in London. With their grandmother."

"And your husband? Is he down? What's he doing this morning? Playing golf?"

She stared at him, accepting for the first time the fact that personal tragedy is just that. Personal. Your own existence could fall to pieces but that did not mean that the rest of the world necessarily knew about it, or even bothered. There was no reason for Eustace to know.

She laid her hands on the edge of the table, aligning them as though their arrangement were of the utmost importance. She said,

"Anthony's dead." Her hands seemed all at once insubstantial, almost transparent, the wrists too thin, the long almond-shaped nails, painted coral pink, as fragile as petals. She wished suddenly, fervently, that they were not like that, but strong and brown and capable, with dirt engrained, and fingernails worn from gardening and peeling potatoes and scraping carrots. She could feel Eustace's eyes upon her. She could not bear him to be sorry for her.

He said, "What happened?"

"He was killed in a car accident. He was drowned."

"Drowned?"

"We have this river, you see, at Kirkton . . . that's where we live in Scotland. The river runs between the house and the road, you have to go over the bridge. And he was coming home and he skidded, or misjudged the turn, and the car went through the wooden railings and into the river. We'd had a lot of rain, a wet month, and the river was in spate and the car went to the bottom. A diver had to go down . . . with a cable. And the police eventually winched it out . . ." Her voice trailed off.

He said gently, "When?"

"Three months ago."

"Not long."

"No. But there was so much to do, so much to see to. I don't know what's happened to the time. And then I caught this bug—a sort of 'flu, and I couldn't throw it off, so my mother-in-law said that she'd have the children in London and I came down here to stay with Alice."

"When are you going away again?"

"I don't know."

He was silent. After a little he picked up his glass and drained his beer. As he set it down he said, "Have you got a car here?"

"Yes." She pointed. "The blue Triumph."

"Then finish that drink and we'll go back to Penfolda." Virginia turned her head and stared at him. "Well, what's so extraordinary about that? It's dinner time. There are pasties in the oven. Do you want to come back and eat one with me?"

". . . Yes."

"Then come. I've got my Land-Rover. You can follow me."

"All right."

He stood up. "Come along, then."

Chapter 3

SHE HAD BEEN to Penfolda once before, only once, and then in the cool half-light of a spring evening ten years before.

"We've been invited to a party," Alice had announced over lunch that day.

Virginia's mother was immediately intrigued. She was immensely social and with a seventeen-year-old daughter to launch into society one only had to mention a party to capture her attention.

"How very nice! Where? Who with?"

Alice laughed at her. Alice was one of the few people who could laugh at Rowena Parsons and get away with it, but then Alice had known her for years.

"Don't get too excited. It's not really your sort of thing."

"My dear Alice, I don't know what you mean. Explain!"

"Well, it's a couple called Barnet. Amos and Fenella Barnet. You may have heard of him. He's a sculptor, very modern, very *avant-garde*. They've taken one of the old studios in Porthkerris, and they have a great number of rather unconventional children."

Without waiting to hear more Virginia said. "Why don't we go?" They sounded exactly the sort of people she was always longing to meet.

Mrs. Parsons allowed a small frown to show between her beautifully aligned eyebrows. "Is the party in the studio?" she inquired, obviously suspecting doctored drinks and doped cigarettes.

"No, it's out at Lanyon at a farm called Penfolda, some sort of a barbecue on the cliffs. A camp fire and fried sausages . . ." Alice saw that Virginia was longing to go. ". . . I think it might be rather fun."

"I think it sounds terrible," said Mrs. Parsons.

"I didn't think you'd want to come. But Tom and I might go, and we'll take Virginia with us."

Mrs. Parsons turned her cool gaze upon her daughter. "Do you *want* to go to a barbecue?"

Virginia shrugged. "It might be fun." She had learned, long ago, that it never paid to be too enthusiastic about anything.

"Very well," said her mother, helping herself to lemon pudding. "If it's your idea of an amusing evening and Alice and Tom don't mind taking you along . . . but for heaven's sake wear something warm. It's bound to be freezing. Far too cold, one would have thought, for a picnic."

She was right. It was cold. A clear turquoise evening with the shoulder of Carn Edvor silhouetted black against the western sky and a chill inland wind to nip the air. Driving up the hill out of Porthkerris, Virginia looked back and saw the lights of the town twinkling far below, the ink-black waters of the harbour brimming with shimmering reflections. Across the bay, from the distant headland, the lighthouse sent its warning signal. A flash. A pause. A flash. A longer pause. Be careful. There's danger.

The evening ahead seemed full of possibilities. Suddenly excited, Virginia turned and leaned forward, resting her chin on crossed arms on the back of Alice's seat. The unpremeditated gesture was clumsy and spontaneous, a reflection of natural high spirits that were normally battened firmly down under the influence of a domineering mother.

"Alice, where is this place we're going?"

"Penfolda. It's a farm, just this side of Lanyon."

"Who lives there?"

"Mrs. Philips. She's a widow. And her son Eustace."

"What does he do?"

"He farms, silly. I told you it was a farm."

"Are they friends of the Barnets?"

"I suppose they must be. A lot of artists live out around this part of the world. Though I've no idea how they could ever have met."

Tom said, "Probably at The Mermaid's."

"What's The Mermaid's?" Virginia asked.

"The Mermaid's Arms, the pub in Lanyon. On a Saturday night all the world and his wife go there for a drink and a get-together."

"Who else will be at the party?"

"Our guess is probably as good as yours."

"Haven't you *any* idea?"

"Well . . ." Alice did her best. ". . . Artists and writers and poets and hippies and drop-outs and farmers and perhaps one or two rather boring and conventional people like us."

Virginia gave her a hug. "You're not boring or conventional. You're super."

"You may not think we're quite so super at the end of the evening. You may hate it, so grit your teeth and reserve your judgment."

Virginia sat back, in the darkness of the car, hugging herself. *I shan't hate it.*

There were headlights like fireflies, coming from all directions, converging on Penfolda. From the road the farmhouse could be seen to be blazing with light. They joined the queue of assorted vehicles which bumped and groaned their way down a narrow, broken land and eventually were directed into a farmyard which had been turned temporarily into a car park. The air was full of voices and laughter as friends greeted friends, and already a steady trickle of people were making their way over a stone wall and down over the pasture fields towards the cliffs. Some were wrapped in rugs, some carried old-fashioned lanterns, some—Virginia was glad all over again that her mother had not come—a clanking bottle or two.

Someone said, "Tom! What are you doing here?", and Tom and Alice dropped back to wait for their friends, and Virginia went on, loving the feeling of being alone. All about her the soft, dark air smelled of peat and sea-wrack and wood-smoke. The sky was not yet empty of light and the sea was of so dark a blue that it was almost black. She went through a gap in a wall and saw, below her, at the bottom of the field, the golden flames of the fire, already ringed with lanterns and the shapes and shadows of about thirty people. As she came closer, faces sprang suddenly into focus, illuminated in firelight, laughing and talking, everybody knowing everybody. There was a barrel of beer, propped on a wooden stand, from which brimming glasses were being continually filled, and there was the smell of potatoes cooking and burning fat, and somebody had brought a guitar and begun to play and gradually a few people gathered about him and raised uncertain voices in song.

> There is a ship
> And she sails the sea,
> She's loaded deep
> As deep can be.
> But not as deep
> As the love I'm in . . .

A young man, running to pass Virginia, stumbled in the dusk and bumped into her. "Sorry." He grabbed her arm, as much to steady himself as her. He held his lantern high, the light in her face. "Who are you?"

"Virginia."

"Virginia who?"

"Virginia Parsons."

He had long hair and a band around his forehead and looked like an Apache.

"I thought it was a new face. Are you on your own?"

"N . . . no. I've come with Alice and Tom . . . but . . ." She looked back. "I've lost them . . . they're coming . . . somewhere . . ."

"I'm Dominic Barnet . . ."

"Oh . . . it's your party . . ."

"No, my father's, really. At least he's paid for the barrel of beer which makes it his party and my mother bought the sausages. Come on . . . let's get something to drink," and he grabbed her arm with an even firmer grip and marched her down into the seething, noisy firelit circle of activity. "Hey, Dad . . . here's someone who hasn't got a drink . . ."

A huge bearded figure, medieval in the strange light, straightened up from the tap of the barrel. "Well, here's one for her," he said, and Virginia found herself holding an enormous mug of beer. "And here's a sausage." The young man whisked one nearly off a passing tray and handed it to her, impaled on a stick. Virginia took that too, and was just about to embark upon some polite social conversation when Dominic saw another familiar face across the circle of firelight, yelled "Mariana!" or some such name, and was away, leaving Virginia once more alone.

She searched in the darkness for the Lingards but could not find them. But everyone else was sitting, so she sat too, with the enormous beer mug in one hand and the sausage, still too hot to eat, in the other. The firelight scorched her face and the wind was cold on her back and blew her hair all over her face. She took a mouthful of beer. She had never drunk beer before and immediately wanted to sneeze. She did so, enormously and from behind her an amused voice said, "Bless you."

Virginia recovered from the sneeze and said, "Thank you," and looked up to see who had blessed her, and saw a large young man in corduroys and rubber boots and a massive Norwegian sweater. He was grinning down at her and the firelight turned his brown face to the colour of copper.

She said, "It was the beer that made me sneeze."

He squatted beside her, took the mug gently from her hand and laid it on the ground between them. "You might sneeze again and then you'd spill it all and that would be a waste."

"Yes."

"You have to be a friend of the Barnets."

"Why do you say that?"

"I haven't seen you before."

"No, I'm not. I came with the Lingards."

"Alice and Tom? Are they here?"

"Yes, somewhere."

He sounded so pleased that the Lingards were here that Virginia fully expected him to go, then and there, in search of them, but instead he settled himself more comfortably on the grass beside her, and seemed quite happy to remain silent, simply watching in some amusement, the rest of the party. Virginia ate her sausage, and when she had finished and he still had said nothing, she decided that she would try again.

"Are you a friend of the Barnets?"

"Um . . ." His attention interrupted, he turned to look at her, his eyes a clear and unwinking blue. "Sorry?"

"I wondered if you were a friend of the Barnets, that's all."

He laughed. "I'd better be. These are my fields they're desecrating."

"Then you must be Eustace Philips."

He considered this. "Yes," he said at last. "I suppose I must be."

Soon after that he was called away . . . some of his Guernseys had wandered in from a neighbouring field and a batty girl who had drunk too much wine thought that she was being attacked by a bull and had thrown a pretty fit of hysterics. So Eustace went to put the matter to rights, and Virginia was presently claimed by Alice and Tom, and although she spent the rest of the evening watching out for him, she did not see Eustace Philips again.

The party, however, was a wild and memorable success. Near midnight, with the beer finished, and the bottles going round, and the food all eaten and the fire piled with driftwood until the flames sprang twenty feet high or more, Alice suggested gently that perhaps it might be a good idea if they went home.

"Your mother will be sitting up thinking you've either been raped or fallen into the sea. And Tom's got to be at the office at nine in the morning and it really is getting bitterly cold. What do you say? Have you had enough? Have you had fun?"

"Such fun," said Virginia, reluctant to leave.

But it was time to go. They walked in silence, away from the firelight and the noise, up the slopes of the fields towards the farm-house.

Now, only one light burned from a downstairs window, but a full moon, white as a plate, sailed high in the sky, filling all the night with silver light. As they came over the wall into the farmyard, a door in the house opened, yellow light spilled out over the cobbles, and a voice called out across the darkness. "Tom! Alice! Come and have a cup of tea or coffee—something to warm you up before you go home."

"Hallo, Eustace." Tom went towards the house. "We thought you'd gone to bed."

"I'm not staying down on the cliffs till dawn, that's for certain. Would you like a drink?"

"I'd like a whisky," said Tom.

"And I'd like tea," said Alice. "What a good idea! We're frozen. Are you sure it's not too much trouble?"

"My mother's still up, she'd like to see you. She's got the kettle on . . ."

They all went into the house, into a low-ceilinged, panelled hall, with a flagged slate floor covered with bright rugs. The beams of the roof scarcely cleared the top of Eustace Philips's head.

Alice was unbuttoning her coat. "Eustace, have you met Virginia? She's staying with us at Wheal House."

"Yes, of course—we said hallo," but he scarcely looked at her. "Come into the kitchen, it's the warmest place in the house. Mother, here are the Lingards. Alice wants a cup of tea. And Tom wants whisky and . . ." He looked down at Virginia. "What do you want?"

"I'd like tea."

Alice and Mrs. Philips at once busied themselves, Mrs. Philips with the teapot and the kettle, and Alice taking cups and saucers down from the shelves of the painted dresser. As they did this they discussed the Barnets's party, laughing about the girl who thought the cow was a bull, and the two men settled themselves at the scrubbed kitchen table with tumblers and a soda siphon and a bottle of Scotch.

Virginia sat too, wedged into the broad window-set at the head of the table, and listening to, without actually hearing, the pleasant blur of voices. She found that she was very sleepy, dazed by the warmth and comfort of the Penfolda kitchen after the bitter cold of the outdoors, and slightly fuzzy from the unaccustomed draught beer.

Sunk into the folds of her coat, hands deep in its pockets, she looked about her and decided that never had she been in a room so welcoming, so secure. There were beams in the ceiling, with old iron hooks for smoking hams, and deep window-sills crammed with flowering geraniums. There was a huge stove where the kettle simmered, and a cane chair with a cat curled in its seat, and there was a Grain Merchant's calendar and curtains of checked cotton and the warm smell of baking bread.

Mrs. Philips was small as her son was large, grey-haired, very neat. She looked as though she had never stopped working from the day she was born and would have it no other way, and as she and Alice moved about the kitchen, deft and quick, gossiping gently about the unconventional Barnets, Virginia watched her and wished that she could have had a mother just like that. Calm and good-humoured with a great comforting kitchen and a kettle always on the boil for a cup of tea.

The tea made, the two women finally joined the others around the table. Mrs. Philips poured a cup for Virginia and handed it to her, and Virginia sat up, pulling her hands out of her pockets and took it, remembering to say "Thank you."

Mrs. Philips laughed. "You're sleepy," she said.

"I know," said Virginia. They were all looking at her, but she stirred her tea and would not look up because she did not want to have to meet that blue and disconcerting gaze.

But eventually it was time to go. With their coats on again, they stood, crowded in the little hallway. The Lingards and Mrs. Philips were already at the open front door when Eustace spoke from behind Virginia.

"Goodbye," he said.

"Oh." Confused, she turned. "Goodbye." She began to put out her hand, but perhaps he did not see it, for he did not take it. "Thank you for letting me come."

He looked amused. "It was a pleasure. You'll have to come back again, another time."

And all the way home, she hugged his words close as though they were a marvellous present that he had given her. But she never came back to Penfolda.

Until today, ten years later, and a July afternoon of piercing beauty. Roadside ditches brimmed with ragged robin and bright yellow coltsfoot, the gorse was aflame and the bracken of the cliff-tops lay emerald against a summer sea the colour of hyacinths.

So engrossed had she been in her business of the day, collecting keys, and finding the cottage at Bosithick, and considering such practical questions as cookers and fridges and bedclothes and china, that all the heaven-sent morning had somehow gone unnoticed. But now it was part of what had suddenly happened and Virginia remembered long ago, how the lighthouse had flashed out over the dark sea, and she had been, for no apparent reason, suddenly excited and warm with a marvellous anticipation.

But you're not seventeen any longer. You're a woman, twenty-seven years old and independent, with two children and a car and a house in Scotland. Life doesn't hold those sort of surprises any longer. Everything is different. Nothing ever stays the same.

At the top of the lane which led down to Penfolda was a wooden platform for the milk churns, and the way sloped steep and winding between high stone walls. Hawthorns leaned distorted by the winter winds, and as Virginia followed the back of Eustace's Land-Rover around the corner of the house, two collies appeared, black and white, barking and raising a din that sent the brown Leghorn hens squawking and scuttling for shelter.

Eustace had parked his Land-Rover in the shade of the barn and was already out of it, toeing the dogs gently out of the way. Virginia put her car behind his and got out as well, and the collies instantly made for her, barking and leaping about and trying to put their front paws on her knees and stretching up to lick her face.

"Get down . . . get down, you devils!"

"I don't mind . . ." She fondled their slim heads, their thick coats. "What are their names?"

"Beaker and Ben. That's Beaker and this is Ben . . . shut up, you, boy! They do this every time . . ."

His manner was robust and cheerful as though during the course of the short drive he had decided that this was the best attitude to adopt if the rest of the day was not to become a sort of wake for Anthony Keile. And Virginia, who did not in the least want this to happen, gratefully took her cue from him. The dogs' noisy welcome helped to break the ice, and it was in an entirely natural and easy fashion that they all went up the cobbled path together, and into the house.

She saw the beams, the flagged floor, the rugs. Unchanged.

"I remember this."

There was a smell of hot pasties, mouth-watering. He went in through the kitchen door, leaving Virginia to follow behind, and across to the stove, whisking an oven cloth off a rack as he passed, and crouching to open the oven.

"They aren't burnt, are they?" she asked anxiously. Fragrant smoky smells issued out.

"No, just right."

He closed the oven door and stood up.

She said, "Did you make them?"

"Me? You must be joking."

"Who did?"

"Mrs. Thomas, my housekeeper . . . like a drink, would you?" He went to open a fridge, to take a can of beer from the inside of the door.

"No, thank you."

He smiled. "I haven't got any Coke."

"I don't want a drink."

As they spoke, Virginia looked about her, terrified that anything in this marvellous room should have been altered, that Eustace might have changed something, moved the furniture, painted the walls. But it was just as she remembered. The scrubbed table pulled into the bay of the window, the geraniums on the window-sills, the dresser packed with bright china. After all these years it remained the epitome of everything a proper kitchen should be, the heart of the house.

When they had taken over Kirkton and were doing it up, cellar to attic, she had tried to get a kitchen like the Penfolda one. Somewhere comfortable and warm where the family would congregate, and drink tea and gossip round the scrubbed table.

"Who wants to go into a kitchen?" Anthony had asked, not understanding at all.

"Everybody. A farmhouse kitchen's like a living-room."

"Well, I'm not going to live in any kitchen, I'll tell you that."

And he ordered stainless steel fitments and bright Formica worktops and a black and white chequered floor that showed every mark and was the devil to keep clean.

Now Virginia leaned against the table and said with deep satisfaction, "I was afraid it would have changed, but it's just the same."

"Why should it have changed?"

"No reason. I was just afraid. Things do change. Eustace, Alice told me that your mother had died . . . I'm sorry."

"Yes. Two years ago. She had a fall. Got pneumonia." He chucked the empty can neatly into a trashbucket and turned to survey her, propping his length against the edge of the sink. "And how about your own mother?"

His voice held no expression; she could detect no undertones of sarcasm or dislike.

"She died, Eustace. She became very ill a couple of years after Anthony and I were married. It was dreadful, because she was ill for so long. And it was difficult, because she was in London and I was at Kirkton . . . I couldn't be with her all the time."

"And I suppose you were all the family she had?"

"Yes. That was part of the trouble. I used to visit her as often as I could, but in the end we had to bring her up to Scotland, and eventually she went into a nursing home in Relkirk, and she died there."

"That's bad."

"Yes. And she was so young. It's a funny thing when your mother dies. You never really grow up till that happens." She amended this. "At least, I suppose that's how some people feel. You were grown up long before then."

"I don't know about that," said Eustace. "But I know what you mean."

"Anyway, it was all over years ago. Don't let's talk about miserable things. Tell me about you, and Mrs. Thomas. Do you know, Alice

Lingard said you'd either have a domesticated mistress or a sexy house-keeper? I can't wait to meet her."

"Well, you'll have to. She's gone to Penzance to see her sister."

"Does she live at Penfolda?"

"She has the cottage at the other end of the house. This used to be three cottages, you know, in the old days, before my grandfather bought the place. Three families lived here and farmed a few acres. Probably had half a dozen cows for milking and sent their sons down the tin mines to keep the wolf from the door."

"Two days ago," said Virginia, "I drove out to Lanyon and sat on the hill, and there were combine harvesters out, and men haymaking. I thought one of them was probably you."

"Probably was."

She said, "I thought you'd be married."

"I'm not."

"I know. Alice Lingard said that you weren't."

After he had finished his beer, he took knives and forks from a drawer and began to lay the table but Virginia stopped him. "It's too nice indoors. Couldn't we eat the pasties in the garden?"

Eustace looked amazed, but said, "All right," and found her a basket for the knives and forks and plates and the salt and pepper and glasses, and he eased the piping hot pasties out of the oven on to a great flowered china dish, and they went out of a side door into the sunshine and the untidy little farmhouse garden. The grass needed cutting and the flower-beds were brimming with cheerful cottage flowers, and there was a washing line, flapping with bright white sheets and pillow-cases.

Eustace had no garden furniture so they sat on the grass, tall with daisies and plantains, with the dishes of their picnic spread about them.

The pasties were enormous, and Virginia had only eaten half of hers, and was defeated by the remainder, by the time that Eustace, propped on an elbow, had consumed the whole length of his.

She said. "I can't eat any more," and gave him the rest of hers, which he took and placidly demolished. He said, through a mouthful of pastry and potato: "If I weren't so hungry, I'd make you eat it, fatten you up a bit."

"I don't want to be fat."

"But you're much too thin. You were always small enough, but now you look as though a puff of wind would blow you away. And you've cut your hair. It used to be long, right down your back, flowing about in the wind." He put out a hand and circled her wrist with his thumb and forefinger. "There's nothing of you."

"Perhaps it was the 'flu."

"I thought you'd be enormous after all these years of eating porridge and herrings and haggis."

"You mean, that's what people eat in Scotland."

"It's what I've been told." He let go of her wrist and peacefully finished the pasty, and then began to collect the plates and the basket and carry everything indoors. Virginia made movements as though to help, but he told her to stay where she was, so she did this, lying back in the grass and staring at the straight grey roof on the barn, and the seagulls perched there, and the scudding shapes of small, white fine-weather clouds, blown from the sea across the incredibly blue sky.

Eustace returned, carrying cigarettes and green eating apples and a Thermos of tea. Virginia lay where she was, and he tossed her an apple and she caught it, and he sat beside her again, unscrewing the cap of the Thermos.

"Tell me about Scotland."

Virginia turned the apple, cool and smooth, in her hands.

"What shall I tell you?"

"What did your husband do?"

"How do you mean?"

"Didn't he have a job?"

"Not exactly. Not a nine-to-five job. But he'd been left this estate . . ."

"Kirkton?"

". . . Yes, Kirkton . . . by an uncle. A great big house and about a thousand acres of land, and after we'd got the house in order, that seemed to take up most of his time. He grew trees, and farmed in a rather gentlemanly way . . . I mean, he had a grieve—a bailiff you'd call him—who lived in the farmhouse. Mr. McGregor. It was he who really did most of the work, but Anthony was always occupied. I mean . . ." she finished feebly . . . "he seemed to be able to fill in his days."

Shooting five days a week in the season, fishing and playing golf. Driving north for the stalking, taking off for St. Moritz for a couple of months every winter. It was no good trying to explain a man like

Anthony Keile to a man like Eustace Philips. They belonged to different worlds.

"And what about Kirkton now?"

"I told you, the grieve looks after it."

"And the house?"

"It's empty. At least, the furniture's all there, but there's nobody living in it."

"Are you going back to this empty house?"

"I suppose so. Some time."

"What about the children?"

"They're in London, with Anthony's mother."

"Why aren't they with you?" asked Eustace, sounding not critical, merely curious, as though he simply wished to know.

"It just seemed a good idea, my coming away on my own. Alice Lingard wrote and asked me to come, and it seemed a good idea, that's all."

"Why didn't you bring the children too?"

"Oh, I don't know . . ." Even to herself her own voice sounded elaborately casual, unconvincing. "Alice doesn't have any children and her house isn't geared for them . . . I mean, everything's rather special and rare and breakable. You know how it is."

"In fact, I don't, but go on."

"Anyway, Lady Keile likes having them with her . . ."

"Lady Keile?"

"Anthony's mother. And Nanny likes going there because she used to work for Lady Keile. She was Anthony's own Nanny when he was a little boy."

"But I thought the children were quite big."

"Cara's eight and Nicholas is six."

"But why do they have to have a Nanny? Why can't you look after them?"

Over the years Virginia had asked herself that question time without number, and had come up with no sort of an answer, but for Eustace to voice it, unasked, out of the blue, filled her with a perverse resentment.

"What do you mean?"

"Just what I say."

"I do look after them. I mean, I see a lot of them . . ."

"If they've just lost their father, surely the one person they need to be with is their mother, not a grandmother and an old inherited Nanny. They'll think everybody's deserting them."

"They won't think anything of the sort."

"If you're so sure, why are you getting so hot under the collar?"

"Because I don't like you interfering, airing your opinions about something you know nothing about."

"I know about you."

"What about me?"

"I know your infinite capacity for being pushed around."

"And who pushes me around?"

"I wouldn't know for sure." She realized with some astonishment that, in a cold way, he was becoming as angry as she. "But at a rough guess I would say your mother-in-law. Perhaps she took over where your own mother left off?"

"Don't you dare to speak about my mother like that."

"But it's true, isn't it?"

"No, it's not true."

"Then get your children down here. It's inhuman leaving them in London for the summer holidays, in weather like this, when they should be running wild by the sea and in the fields. Take your finger out, ring up your mother-in-law and tell her to put them on a train. And if Alice Lingard doesn't want them at Wheal House, because she's afraid of the ornaments getting broken, then take them to a pub, or rent a cottage . . ."

"That's exactly what I intend doing, and I didn't need you to tell me."

"Then you'd better start looking for one."

"I already have."

He was momentarily silenced, and she thought with satisfaction: That took the wind out of his sails.

But only momentarily. "Have you found anything?"

"I looked at one house this morning but it was impossible."

"Where?"

"Here. In Lanyon." He waited for her to tell him. "It was called Bosithick," she added ungraciously.

"Bosithick!" He appeared delighted. "But that's a marvellous house."

"It's a terrible house"

"Terrible?" He could not believe his ears. "You do mean the cottage up the hill where Aubrey Crane used to live? The one that the Kernows inherited from his old aunt."

"That's the one, and it's creepy and quite impossible."

"What does creepy mean? Haunted?"

"I don't know. Just creepy."

"If it's haunted by the ghost of Aubrey Crane you might have quite an amusing time. My mother remembered him, said he was a dear man. And very fond of children," he added with what seemed to Virginia a classic example of a *non sequitur.*

"I don't care what sort of a man he was, I'm not going to take the house."

"Why not?"

"Because I'm not."

"Give me three good reasons . . ."

Virginia lost her patience. "Oh, for heaven's sake . . ." She made as if to get to her feet, but Eustace, with unexpected speed for such a large man, caught her wrist in his hand and pulled her back on to the grass. She looked angrily into his eyes and saw them cold as blue stones.

"Three good reasons," he said again.

She looked down at his hand on her arm. He made no effort to move it and she said, "There's no fridge."

"I'll lend you a meat-safe. Reason number two."

"I told you. It's got a spooky atmosphere. The children have never lived anywhere like that. They'd be frightened."

"Not unless they're as hen-brained as their mother. Now, number three."

Desperately she tried to think up some good, watertight reason, something that would convince Eustace of her nameless horror of the odd little house on the hill. But all she came out with was a string of petty excuses, each sounding more feeble than the last. "It's too small, and it's dirty, and where would I wash the children's things, and I don't even know it there's an iron for the ironing or a lawn-mower to cut the grass. And there's no garden, just a sort of washing green place, and inside all the furniture is so depressing and . . ."

He interrupted her. "These aren't reasons, Virginia, and you know they're not. They're just a lot of bloody excuses."

"Bloody excuses for *what*?"

"For not having a show-down with your mother-in-law or the old

Nanny or possibly both. For making a scene and asserting yourself and bringing your own children up the way you want them to go."

Fury at him caught in her throat, a great lump that rendered her speechless. She felt the blood surge to her cheeks, she began to tremble, but although he must have seen all this, he went calmly on, saying all the terrible things that the voice in the back of her head had been saying for years, but to which she had never had the moral courage to pay any attention.

"I don't think you can give a damn for your children. You don't want to be bothered with them. Someone else has always done the washing and the ironing and you're not going to start now. You're too bloody idle to take them for picnics and read them books and put them to bed. It's really nothing to do with Bosithick. Whatever house you found, you'd be sure to find something wrong with it. Any excuse would do provided you never have to admit to yourself that you can't be bloody bothered to take care of your own children."

Before the last word was out of his mouth, she was on her feet, tearing her arm free of his grip.

"It's not true! It's none of it true! I do want them! I've been wanting them ever since I got here . . . !"

"Then get them here, you little fool . . ." He was on his feet too, and they were shouting at each other across three feet of grass as though it were a desert.

"That's what I'm going to do. That's just exactly what I'm going to do."

"I'll believe that when you do it!"

She turned and fled and was into her car before she remembered her handbag, still lying on the kitchen table. By now in floods of tears, she was out of the car and running into the house to retrieve it before Eustace reached her again. Then back to the car and turning it furiously, dangerously in the narrow confines of the farmyard, then back up the lane, with a roar of the engine and a great spattering of loose gravel from the back wheels.

"Virginia!"

Through tears, through the driving-mirror she saw him standing far behind her. She jammed her foot on the accelerator and swung out on to the main road without bothering to wait and see if anything was coming. By good chance it wasn't, but she didn't slow down all the way back to Porthkerris, down into the town and up the other side, parking the car on the double yellow lines outside the solicitors' office and leaving it there while she ran inside.

This time she did not ring the bell, nor wait for Miss Leddra, but went, like the wind, through the outer office to fling open wide the door of Mr. Williams's room, where Mr. Williams was rudely interrupted in the course of interviewing an autocratic old lady from Truro about the seventh set of alterations to her will.

Both Mr. Williams and the old lady, silenced by astonishment, stared, open-mouthed. Mr. Williams, recovering first, began to scramble to his feet. "Mrs. Keile!" But before he could say another word Virginia had flung the keys of Bosithick on to his desk and said, "I'll take it. I'll take it right away. And as soon's I've got my children, I'm moving in!"

Chapter 4

ALICE SAID, "I'm sorry Virginia, but I think you're making the most terrible mistake. What's more, it's a classic mistake and one so many people make when they suddenly find themselves alone in the world. You're acting on impulse, you haven't really thought about this at all . . ."

"I have thought about it."

"But the children are fine, you know they are, settled and happy with Nanny and your mother-in-law. The life they're leading is simply an extension of life at Kirkton, all the things they know and that helps them to feel secure. Their father's dead, and nothing's ever going to be the same for them again. But if there have to be changes, at least let them happen slowly, gradually; let Cara and Nicholas have time to get used to them."

"They're my children."

"But you've never looked after them. You've never had them on your own, except the odd times when Nanny could be persuaded to take a holiday. They'll exhaust you, and honestly, Virginia, at the moment I don't think you're physically capable of doing it. After all, that's why you came here, to recuperate from that loathsome 'flu, and generally have a little peace and quiet, give yourself time to get over the bad things that have been happening. Don't deprive yourself of that. You're going to need all your resources when you do eventually go back to Kirkton and start picking up the threads and learning to live without Anthony."

"I'm not going to Kirkton. I'm going to Bosithick. I've already paid the first week's rent."

Alice's expression stopped being patient and became exasperated.

"But it's so ridiculous! Look, if you feel so strongly about having the children down here, then have them by all means, they can stay here, but for heaven's sake let Nanny come too."

Only yesterday the idea could have been tempting. But now Virginia never even let herself consider it.

"I've made up my mind."

"But why didn't you *tell* me? Why didn't you discuss it with me?"

"I don't know. It was just something I had to do on my own."

"And where *is* Bosithick?"

"It's on the Lanyon road . . . You can't see it from the road, but it's got a sort of tower . . ."

"The place where Aubrey Crane lived? But, Virginia, it's ghastly. There's nothing there but moor and wind and cliffs. You'll be totally isolated!"

Virginia tried to turn it into a joke. "You'll have to come and see me. Make sure the children and I aren't driving each other slowly insane."

But Alice did not laugh, and Virginia, seeing her frown and the disapproving set of her mouth, was suddenly, astonishingly reminded of her own mother. It was as though Alice was no longer Virginia's contemporary, her friend, but had swung back a generation and from that lofty height was telling the young Virginia that she was being a fool. But perhaps, after all, this was not so strange. She had known Rowena Parsons long before Virginia was born, and the fact that she had no children of her own to contend with meant that her attitudes and opinions remained rigidly unchanged.

She said at last, "It isn't that I want to interfere, you know that. But I've known you all your life, and I can't stand to one side and watch you do this insane thing."

"What's so insane about having your children on holiday with you?"

"It's not just that, Virginia, and you know it. If you take them away from Lady Keile and Nanny without their approval, which I doubt very much you'll get, there's going to be one devil of a row."

Virginia felt sick at the thought of it. "Yes, I know."

"Nanny will probably take the most terrible umbrage and give in her notice."

"I know . . ."

"Your mother-in-law will do everything she can to stop you."

"I know that too."

Alice stared at her, as though she were staring at a stranger. Then suddenly, she shrugged and laughed, in a hopeless sort of way. "I don't understand. What made you suddenly so determined?"

Virginia had said nothing about her encounter with Eustace Philips and had no intention of doing so.

"Nothing. Nothing in particular."

"It must be the sea air," said Alice. "Extraordinary what it does for people." She picked a fallen newspaper off the floor, began folding it meticulously. "When are you going to London?"

"Tomorrow."

"And Lady Keile?"

"I'll phone her tonight. And Alice, I am sorry. And thank you for being so kind."

"I haven't been kind, I've been critical and disapproving. But somehow, I always think of you as someone young and helpless. I feel responsible for you."

"I'm twenty-seven. And I'm not helpless. And I'm responsible for myself."

Nanny answered the telephone. "Yes?"

"Nanny?"

"Yes."

"It's Mrs. Keile."

"Oh, hallo! Do you want to speak to Lady Keile?"

"Is she there? . . ."

"Just a moment and I'll get her."

"Nanny."

"Yes."

"How are the children?"

"Oh, they're very well. Having a lovely time. Just gone to bed." (This was slipped in quickly in case Virginia should ask to speak to them.)

"Is it hot?"

Oh, yes. Lovely. Perfect weather. Hold on and I'll tell Lady Keile you're there."

There were the sounds of Nanny putting down the receiver, her footsteps going across the hall, her distant voice. "Lady Keile!"

Virginia waited. *If I was a woman who was taking to drink I would have one in my hand, right now. A great tall tumbler of dark-coloured whisky.* But she wasn't and her stomach lay heavy with impending doom.

More footsteps, sharp neat, unmistakable. The receiver was lifted once more.

"Virginia."

"Yes, it's me."

The situation was hideously complicated by the fact that Virginia had never known what to call her mother-in-law. "Call me Mother," she had said kindly, as soon as Virginia and Anthony were married, but somehow this was impossible. And "Lady Keile" was worse. Virginia had compromised by only corresponding by postcard or telegram, and always calling her "you."

"How nice to hear you, dear. How are you feeling?"

"I'm very well . . ."

"And the weather? I believe you're having a heatwave."

"Yes, it's unbelievable. Look . . ."

"How is Alice?"

"She's very well, too . . ."

"And the darling children, they've been swimming today—the Turners have got a delicious pool in their garden, and invited Cara and Nicholas over for the afternoon. What a pity they're in bed; why didn't you call earlier?"

Virginia said, "I've got something to tell you."

"Yes?"

She closed her hand around the receiver until her knuckles ached. "I've been able to find a little cottage, quite near here. It's near the sea, and I thought it would be nice for the children if they came down and we spent the rest of the holidays together."

She paused, waiting for comment but there was only silence.

"The thing is, the weather is so beautiful and I feel so guilty enjoying it all on my own . . . and it would be good for them to have some sea air before we all have to go back to Scotland and they have to go back to school."

Lady Keile said, "A cottage? But I thought you were staying with Alice Lingard?"

"Yes, I am. I have been. I'm calling from Wheal House now. But I've taken this cottage."

"I don't understand."

"I want the children to come down and spend the rest of the holidays with me. I'll come up tomorrow in the train to fetch them."

"But what sort of a cottage?"

"Just a cottage. A holiday cottage . . ."

"Well, if that's what you want . . ." Virginia began to breathe a sigh of relief. ". . . But it seems hard luck on Nanny. It's not often she gets the chance of being in London and seeing all her own friends." The relief swiftly died. Virginia went back into the attack again.

"Nanny doesn't have to come."

Lady Keile was confused. "I'm sorry, the line's not very clear. I thought you said Nanny didn't have to come."

"She doesn't. I can look after the children. There's not room for her anyway. I mean there isn't a bedroom for her, or a nursery . . . and it's terribly isolated, and she'd hate it."

"You mean you intend taking the children *away* from Nanny?"

"Yes."

"But she'll be most terribly upset."

"Yes, I'm afraid she will, but . . ."

"Virginia . . ." Lady Keile's voice was upset, distressed. "Virginia, we can't talk about this over the telephone."

Virginia imagined Nanny on the upstairs landing, listening to the one-sided conversation.

"We don't need to. I'm coming up to London tomorrow. I'll be with you about five o'clock. We can talk about it then."

"I think," said Lady Keile, "that that would be best."

And she rang off.

The next morning Virginia drove to Penzance, left her car in the station park and caught the train to London. It was another hot, cloudless morning and she had not had time to reserve a seat, and, despite the fact that she managed to get hold of a porter and tip him handsomely, he could only find her an empty corner in a carriage that was already uncomfortably full. Her fellow passengers were going home at the end of their annual holidays, grumpy and disconsolate at the thought of returning to work, and resentful at leaving the sea and the beaches on such a perfect day.

There was a family, a father and mother and two children. The baby slept damply in its mother's arms, but as the sun climbed higher into the unwinking sky and the train rattled northwards through the shimmering heat of a midsummer noon, the elder child became more and more fractious, whining, grizzling, never still, and grinding his dirty sandalled feet on to Virginia's every time he wanted to look out the window. At one point, in order to keep the child quiet, his father bought him an orangeade, but no sooner was the bottle opened than the train lurched and the entire contents went all over the front of Virginia's dress.

The child was promptly slapped by his distracted mother and roared. The baby woke up and added his wails to his brother's. The father said, "Now look what you've done," and gave the child a shake for good measure, and Virginia, trying to mop herself up with face tissues, protested that it didn't matter, it couldn't be helped, it didn't matter at all.

After a good deal of screaming the child subsided into hiccuping sobs. A bottle was produced from somewhere and stuffed into the baby's mouth. It sucked for a bit, and then stopped sucking, struggled into a sitting position and was sick.

And Virginia lit a cigarette and looked firmly out of the window and prayed, "Don't let Cara and Nicholas ever be like that. Don't let them ever be like that on a railway journey, otherwise I shall go stark, staring mad."

London was airless and stuffy, the great cavern of Paddington Station hideous with noise and aimless, hurrying crowds. As soon as she was off the train Virginia, carrying her suitcase, and filthy and crumpled in her stained, sticky dress, walked the length of the platform to the booking-office and, like a secret agent making sure of his escape route, bought tickets and reserved three seats on the Riviera for the following morning. Only then did she return to the taxi rank, wait in the long queue, and finally capture a cab to take her home.

"Thirty-two Melton Gardens, please. Kensington."

"OK. 'op in."

They went down by Sussex Gardens, across the park. The brown grass was littered with picnicking families, children in scanty clothes, couples entwined beneath the shade of trees. In Brompton Road there were window boxes bright with flowers, shop windows filled with clothes "For Cruising," the first of the rush hour crowds was being sucked, a steady stream of humanity, down Knightsbridge Underground.

The cab turned into the network of quiet squares that lay behind

Kensington High Street, edged down narrow roads lined with parked cars, and finally turned the corner into Melton Gardens.

"It's the house by the pillar box."

The taxi stopped. Virginia got out, put her case on the pavement, opened her bag for the fare. The driver said, "Thanks very much," and snapped up his flag, and Virginia picked up her case and turned towards the house and, as she did so, the black-painted door opened and her mother-in-law waited to let her in.

She was tall, slim, immensely good-looking. Even on this breathless day she looked cool and uncrushed, not a wrinkle in her linen dress, not a hair out of place.

Virginia went up the steps towards her.

"How clever of you to know I was here."

"I was looking out of the drawing-room window. I saw the taxi."

Her expression was friendly, smiling, but quite implacable, like the matron of a lunatic asylum come to admit a new patient. They kissed, touching cheeks.

"Did you have a terrible journey?" She closed the door behind them. The cool, pale-coloured hall smelt of beeswax and roses. At the far end steps led down to the glass side door, and beyond it could be seen the garden, the chestnut tree, the children's swing.

"Yes, it was ghastly. I feel filthy and a revolting child spilt orange juice all over me." The house was silent. "Where are the children?"

Lady Keile began to lead the way upstairs to the drawing-room. "They're out with Nanny. I thought perhaps it would be better. They won't be long, not more than half an hour. That should give us time to get this all thrashed out."

Treading behind her, Virginia said nothing. Lady Keile reached the top of the stairs, crossed the small landing and went in through the drawing-room door and Virginia followed her, and, despite her anxiety of mind, was struck, as always, by the timeless beauty of the room, the perfect proportions of the long windows which faced out over the street, open today, the fine net curtains stirring. There were long mirrors, filling the room with reflected light and these gave back images of highly polished antique furniture, tall cabinets of blue and white Meissen plates, and the flowers with which Lady Keile had always surrounded herself.

They faced each other across the pale, fitted carpet. Lady Keile said, "We may as well be comfortable," and lowered herself, straight as a ramrod, into a formal, wide-lapped French chair.

Virginia sat too, on the very edge of the sofa, and tried not to feel like a domestic servant being interviewed for a job. She said, "There really isn't anything to thrash out, you know."

"I thought I must have misunderstood you on the telephone last night."

"No, you didn't misunderstand me. I decided two days ago that I wanted the children with me. I decided it was ridiculous, me being in Cornwall and them in London, specially during the summer holidays. So I went to a solicitor and I found this little house. And I've paid the rent and I've got the keys. I can move in right away."

"Does Alice Lingard know about this?"

"Of course. And she offered to have the children at Wheal House, but by then I'd committed myself and couldn't go back."

"But Virginia, you *surely* can't mean that you want them without Nanny?"

"Yes, I do."

"But you'll never manage."

"I shall have to try."

"What you mean is that you want the children to yourself."

"Yes."

"Are you sure you aren't being a little . . . selfish?"

"*Selfish?*"

"Yes, selfish. You're not thinking of the children, are you? Only yourself."

"Perhaps I am thinking of myself, but I'm thinking of the children too."

"You can't be if you intend taking them away from Nanny."

"Have you spoken to her?"

"I had to, of course. She had to have some idea of what I understood you wanted to do. But I hoped I would be able to change your mind."

"What did she say?"

"She didn't say very much. But I could tell that she was very upset."

"Yes, I'm sure."

"You must think of Nanny, Virginia. Those children are her life. You must consider her."

"With the best will in the world I don't see that she comes into this."

"Of course she comes into it. She comes into everything that we do. Why, she's family, she's been part of the family for years, ever since Anthony was a tiny boy . . . and the way she's looked after those babies of yours, she's devoted herself, given her life to them. And you say she doesn't come into this."

"She wasn't my Nanny," said Virginia. "She didn't look after me when I was a little girl. You can't expect me to feel quite the same about her as you do."

"You really mean to say you feel no sort of loyalty towards her? After letting her bring up your children? After virtually living with her for eight years at Kirkton? I must say you fooled me. I always thought there was a very happy atmosphere between you."

"If there was a happy atmosphere it was because of me. It was because I gave in to Nanny over every little thing, just to keep the peace. Because if she didn't get her own way, she would go into a sulk that would last for days, and I simply couldn't bear it."

"I always imagined you were the mistress of your own home."

"Well, you were wrong. I wasn't. And even if I'd plucked up the courage to have a row with Nanny, and asked her to leave, Anthony would never have heard of it. He thought the sun rose and fell on her head."

At the mention of her son's name Lady Keile had gone a little pale. Her shoulders were consciously straight, her clasped hands tightened in her lap. She said, icily, "And I suppose now that no longer has to be considered."

Virginia was instantly repentant. "I didn't mean that. You know I didn't mean that. But I'm left now. I'm on my own. The children are all I have. Perhaps I'm being selfish, but I need them. I need them so badly with me. I've missed them so much since I've been away."

Outside, across the street, a car drew up, a man began to argue, a woman answered him in anger, her voice shrill with annoyance. As though the noise were more than she could stand, Lady Keile stood up and went over to close the window.

She said, "I shall miss them too."

If we had ever been close, thought Virginia, I could go now and put my arms around her and give her the comfort she is longing for.

But it was not possible. Affection had existed between them, and respect. But never love, never familiarity.

"Yes, I'm sure you will. You've been so wonderfully good to them, and to me. And I'm sorry."

Her mother-in-law turned from the window, brisk again, emotion controlled. "I think," she said, making for the bell-pull which hung at the side of the fireplace, "that it would be a good idea if we were to have a cup of tea."

The children returned at half past five. the front door opened and shut and their voices rose from the hall. Virginia laid down her tea-cup and sat quite still. Lady Keile waited until the footsteps had passed the landing outside the drawing-room door and were on their way upstairs to the nursery. Then she got up and went across the drawing-room and opened the door.

"Cara. Nicholas."

"Hallo, Granny."

"There is someone here to see you."

"Who?"

"A lovely surprise. Come and see."

Much later, after the children had gone upstairs for their bath and supper, after Virginia herself had bathed and changed into a clean cool silk dress, and before the gong rang for dinner, she went upstairs to the nursery to see Nanny.

She found her alone, tidying away the children's supper things and straightening the room before she settled to her nightly session with the television.

Not that the room needed straightening, but Nanny could not relax until every cushion was plump and straight on the sofa, every toy put away, and the children's dirty clothes discarded, and clean ones set out for the following morning. She had always been like this, revelling in the orderly pattern of her own rigid routine. And she had always looked the same, a neat spare woman, over sixty now, but with scarcely a trace of grey in her dark hair which she wore drawn back and fastened in a bun. She appeared to be ageless, the type that would continue, unchanging, until she was an old woman when she would suddenly become senile and die.

She looked up as Virginia came into the room, and then hastily away again.

"Hallo, Nanny."

"Good evening."

Her manner was frigid. Virginia shut the door and went to sit on the arm of the sofa. There was only one way to deal with Nanny in a mood and that was to jump right in off the deep end. "I'm sorry about this, Nanny."

"I don't know what you mean, I'm sure."

"I mean about my taking the children away. We're going back to Cornwall tomorrow morning. I've got seats on the train." Nanny folded the checked tablecloth, corner to corner into perfect squares. "Lady Keile said she'd spoken to you."

"She certainly mentioned something about some hare-brained scheme . . . but it was hard to believe that my ears weren't playing me tricks."

"Are you cross because I'm taking them, or because you're not coming too?"

"Who's cross? Nobody's cross, I'm sure . . ."

"Then you think it's a good idea?"

"No, that I do not. But what I think doesn't seem to matter any more, one way or the other."

She opened a drawer in the table and laid the cloth away, and shut the drawer with a little slam which instantly betrayed her scarcely-banked rage. But her face remained cool, her mouth primly set.

"You know that what you think matters. You've done so much for the children. You mustn't think I'm not grateful. But they're not babies any longer."

"And what is that meant to convey, if I might ask?"

"Just that I can look after them now."

Nanny turned from the table. For the first time, her eyes met Virginia's. And as they watched each other, Virginia saw the slow, angry flush spread up Nanny's neck, up her face, up to her hair line.

She said, "Are you giving me my notice?"

"No, that's not what I intended at all. But perhaps, now we've started to discuss it, it would be the best thing. For your sake as much as anyone else's. Perhaps it would be better for you."

"And why would it be better for me? All my life I've given to this family, why, I had Anthony to look after from the beginning, and there was no reason why I should come up to Scotland and take care of your babies, I never wanted to go, to leave London, but Lady Keile asked me, and because it was the family, I went, a real sacrifice I made, and this is all the thanks I get . . ."

"Nanny . . ." Virginia interrupted gently when Nanny paused for a breath ". . . It would be better for you because of this. For that very reason. Wouldn't it be better to make a clean break, and maybe have a new baby to take care of, a new little family? You know how you always said a nursery wasn't a nursery without a little baby, and Nicholas is six now . . ."

"I never thought I'd live to see the day . . ."

"And if you don't want to do that, then why not speak to Lady Keile? You could maybe make some arrangement with her. You get on so well together, and you like being in London, with all your friends . . ."

"I don't need you to give me any suggestions, thank you very much . . . given up the best years of my life . . . bringing up your children . . . never expected any thanks . . . never would have happened if poor Anthony . . . if Anthony had been alive . . ."

It went on and on, and Virginia sat and listened, letting the invective pour over her. She told herself that this was the least she could do. It was over, it was done, and she was free. Nothing else mattered. To wait, politely, for Nanny to finish was no more than a salute of respect, a tribute paid by the victor to the vanquished after a bloodthirsty but honourable battle.

Afterwards, she went to say good night to the children. Nicholas was already asleep, but Cara was still deep in her book. When her mother came into the room, she looked up slowly, dragging her eyes away from the printed page. Virginia sat on the edge of her bed.

"What are you reading now?"

Cara showed her. "It's *The Treasure Seekers*."

"Oh, I remember that. Where did you find it?"

"In the nursery bookcase."

Carefully, she marked the place in her book with a cross-stitched marker she had made herself, closed it and put it down on her bedside table. "Have you been talking to Nanny?"

"Yes."

"She's been funny all day."

"Has she, Cara?"

"Is something wrong?"

It was hard to be so perceptive, so sensitive to atmosphere when you were only eight years old. Especially when you were shy and not very pretty and had to wear round steel spectacles that made you look like a little owl.

"No, nothing's wrong. Just different. And new."

"What do you mean?"

"Well, I'm going back to Cornwall tomorrow morning in the train, and I'm going to take you and Nicholas with me. Will you like that?"

"You mean . . ." Cara's face lit up. "We're going to stay with Aunt Alice?"

"No, we're going to stay in a house on our own. A funny little house called Bosithick. And we're going to have to do all the house-keeping ourselves and the cooking . . ."

"Isn't Nanny coming?"

"No. Nanny's staying here."

There was a long silence. Virginia said, "Do . . . you mind?"

"No, I don't mind. But I expect she will. That's why she's been so funny."

"It's not easy for Nanny. You and Nicholas have been her babies ever since you were born. But somehow I think you're growing out of Nanny now, like you grow out of coats and dresses . . . You're both old enough to look after yourselves."

"You mean, Nanny's not going to live with us any more?"

"No, she's not."

"Where will she live?"

"She'll maybe go and find another little new baby to take care of. Or she may stay here with Granny."

"She likes being in London," said Cara. "She told me so. She likes it much better than Scotland."

"Well, there you are!"

Cara considered this for a moment. Then she said, "When are we going to Cornwall?"

"I told you. Tomorrow on the train."

"When will we leave?" She liked everything cut and dried.

"About half past nine. We'll get a taxi to the station."

"And when are we going back to Kirkton?"

"I expect when the holidays are over. When you have to go back to school." Cara remained silent. It was impossible to tell what she was thinking. Virginia said, "It's time to go to sleep now . . . we've got a long day tomorrow," and she leaned forward and gently unhooked Cara's spectacles and kissed her good night.

But as she went towards the door, Cara spoke again.

"Mummy."

Virginia turned. "Yes."

"You came."

Virginia frowned, not understanding.

"You came," said Cara again. "I said to write to me, but you came instead."

Virginia remembered the letter from Cara, the catalyst that had started everything off. She smiled. "Yes," she said. "I came. It seemed better." And she went out of the room, and downstairs to endure the ordeal of a silent dinner in the company of Lady Keile.

Chapter 5

Virginia awoke slowly, to a quite unaccustomed mood of achievement. She felt purposeful and strong, two such alien sensations that it was worth lying for a little, quietly, to savour them. Pillowed in Lady Keile's incomparably comfortable spare bed, lapped in hem-stitched linen and cloudy blankets, she watched the early sunshine of another perfect summer morning seep in long strands of gold through the leafy branches of the chestnut tree. The bad things were over, the dreaded hurdles somehow cleared, and in a couple of hours she and the children would be on their way. She told herself that after last night she would never be afraid to tackle anything, no problem was insurmountable, no problem too knotty. She let her imagination move cautiously forward to the weeks ahead, to the pitfalls of coping with Cara and Nicholas single-handed, the discomfort and inconvenience of the little house she had so recklessly rented for them, and still her good spirits remained undismayed. She had turned a corner. From now on everything was going to be different.

It was half past seven. She got up, revelling in the fine weather, the sound of bird-song, the pleasant, distant hum of traffic. She bathed and dressed and packed and stripped her bed and went downstairs.

Nanny and the children always had breakfast in the nursery and Lady Keile hers on a tray in her bedroom, but this was a perfectly ordered household and Virginia found that coffee had been set out for her on the dining-room hot-plate, and a single place laid at the head of the polished table.

She drank two cups of scalding black coffee and ate toast and marmalade. Then she took the key from the table to the hall and let herself out of the front door into the quiet morning streets and walked down to the small old-fashioned grocer's patronized by Lady Keile. There she laid in sufficient provisions to start them off when they eventually got back to Bosithick. Bread and butter and bacon and eggs and coffee and cocoa, and baked beans (which she knew Nicholas adored, but Nanny had never approved of) and tomato soup and choc-olate biscuits. Milk and vegetables they would have to find when they got down there, meat and fish could come later. She paid for all this, and the grocer packed it for her in a stout cardboard carton and she walked back to Melton Gardens with her weighty load carried before her in both arms.

She found the children and Lady Keile downstairs; no sign of Nanny. But the small suitcases, doubtless perfectly packed, were lined up in the hall, and Virginia dumped the carton of groceries down beside them.

"Hallo, Mummy!"

"Hallo." She kissed them both. They were clean and tidy, ready for their journey, Cara in a blue cotton dress and Nicholas in shorts and a striped shirt, his dark hair lately flattened by a hairbrush. "What have you been doing?" he wanted to know.

"I've been buying some groceries. We probably won't have time to go shopping when we get to Penzance; it would be terrible if we didn't have anything to eat."

"I didn't know till this morning when Cara told me. I didn't know till I woke up that we were going in the train."

"I'm sorry. You were asleep last night when I came in to tell you and I didn't want to disturb you."

"I wish you had. I didn't know until *breakfast*." He was very re-sentful.

Smiling at him, Virginia looked up at her mother-in-law. Lady Keile was drawn and pale. Otherwise she looked, as always, perfectly groomed, quite in charge of the situation. Virginia wondered if she had slept at all.

"You should telephone for a taxi," said Lady Keile. "You don't want to risk missing the train. It's always best to be on the early side. There's a number by the telephone."

Wishing that she had thought of this herself Virginia went to do as she was told. The clock in the hall struck a quarter past nine. In ten minutes' time the taxi was there and they were ready to leave.

"But we have to say goodbye to Nanny!" said Cara.

Virginia said, "Yes, of course. Where is Nanny?"

"She's in the nursery." Cara started for the stairs, but Virginia said, "No."

Cara turned and stared, shocked by the unaccustomed tone of her mother's voice.

"But we *have* to say goodbye."

"Of course. Nanny will come down and see you off. I'll go up now and tell her we're just on our way. You get everything together."

She found Nanny determinedly occupied in some entirely unnecessary task.

"Nanny, we're just going."

"Oh, yes."

"The children want to say goodbye."

Silence.

Last night Virginia had been sorry for her, had, in a funny way, respected her. But now all she wanted to do was take Nanny by her shoulders and shake her till her stupid head fell off. "Nanny, this is ridiculous. You can't let it end this way. Come downstairs and say goodbye to them."

It was the first direct order she had ever given to Nanny. The first, she thought, and the last. Like Cara, Nanny was obviously shaken. For a moment she stalled, her mouth worked, she seemed to be trying to think up some excuse. Virginia caught her eye and held it. Nanny tried to stare her out, but was defeated, her eyes slid away. It was the final triumph.

"Very well, madam," said Nanny and followed Virginia back down to the hall, where the children rushed at her in the most gratifying way, hugged her and kissed her as though she were the only person in the world they loved, and then, with this demonstration of affection safely over, ran down the steps and across the pavement and into the waiting taxi.

"Goodbye," said Virginia to her mother-in-law. There was nothing more to be said. They kissed once more, leaning cheeks, kissing the air. "And goodbye, Nanny." But Nanny was already on her way up to the nursery again, fumbling for her handkerchief and blowing her nose. Only her legs were visible, treading upstairs, and the next moment she had reached the turn of the landing and disappeared.

She need have had no fear about her children's behaviour. The novelty of the train journey did not excite, but silenced them. They had not often been taken on holiday, and never to the seaside, and when they travelled to London to stay with their grandmother had been bundled into the night train already dressed in their pyjamas and had slept the journey away.

Now, they stared from the window at the racing countryside as though they had neither of them ever seen fields or farms or cows or towns before. After a little, when the charm of this wore off, Nicholas opened the present Virginia had bought for him at Paddington and smiled with satisfaction when he saw the little red tractor.

He said, "It's like the Kirkton one. Mr. McGregor had a Massey Fergusson just like this." He spun the wheels and made tractor noises in the back of his throat, running the toy up and down the prickly British Railway upholstery.

But Cara did not even open her comic. It lay folded on her lap, and she continued to stare out of the window, her bulging forehead leaning against the glass, her eyes intent behind her spectacles, missing nothing.

At half past twelve they went for lunch and this was another adventure, lurching down the corridor, rushing through the scary connections before the carriages came apart. The dining-car they found enthralling, the tables and the little lights, the indulgent waiter and the grown-upness of being handed a menu.

"And what would madam like?" the waiter asked, and Cara went pink with embarrassed giggles when she realized that he was speaking to her, and had to be helped to order tomato soup and fried fish, and to decide the world-shaking problem of whether she would eat a white ice-cream or a pink.

Watching their faces Virginia thought: Because it's new and exciting to them, it's new and exciting for me. The most trivial, ordinary occurrences will become special because I shall see them through Cara's eyes. And if Nicholas asks me questions that I can't answer, I shall have to go and look them up and I shall become informed and knowledgeable and a brilliant conversationalist.

The idea was funny. She laughed suddenly, and Cara stared and then laughed back, not knowing what the joke was, but delighted to be sharing it with her mother.

* * *

"When did you first come on this train down to Cornwall?" Cara asked.

"When I was seventeen. Ten years ago."

"Didn't you come when you were a little girl my age?"

"No, I didn't. I used to go to an aunt in Sussex."

Now, it was afternoon and they had the compartment to themselves. Nicholas, charmed by the adventure of the corridor, had elected to stay out there, and could be seen straddle-legged, trying to adjust his small weight to the rocking of the train.

"Tell me."

"What? About Sussex?"

"No. About coming to Cornwall."

"Well, we just came. My mother and I, to stay with Alice and Tom Lingard. I'd just left school, and Alice wrote to invite us, and my mother thought it would be nice to have a holiday."

"Was it a summer holiday?"

"No. It was Easter. Spring time. All the daffodils were out and the railway cuttings were thick with primroses."

"Was it hot?"

"Not really. But sunny, and much warmer than Scotland. In Scotland we never really have a proper spring, do we? One day it's winter and the next day all the leaves are out on the trees and it's summer time. At least that's the way it's always seemed to me. In Cornwall the spring is quite a long season . . . that's why they're able to grow all the lovely flowers and send them to Covent Garden to be sold."

"Did you swim?"

"No. The sea would have been icy."

"But in Aunt Alice's pool?"

"She didn't have a pool in those days."

"Will we swim in Aunt Alice's pool?"

"Sure to."

"Will we swim in the sea?"

"Yes, we'll find a lovely beach and swim there."

"I . . . I'm not very good at swimming."

"It's easier in the sea than in ordinary water. The salt helps you to float."

"But don't the waves splash into your face?"

"A little. But that's part of the fun."

Cara considered this. She did not like getting her face wet. With-out her spectacles things became blurred and she couldn't swim with her spectacles on.

"What else did you do?"

"Oh, we used to go out in the car, and go shopping. And if it was warm we used to sit in the garden, and Alice used to have friends to tea, and people for dinner. And sometimes I used to go for walks. There are lovely walks there. Up to the hill behind the house, or down into Porthkerris. The streets are all steep and narrow, so narrow you could scarcely get a car down them. And there were lots of little stray cats, and the harbour, with fishing boats and old men sitting around enjoying the sunshine. And sometimes the tide was in and all the boats were bobbing about in the deep blue water, and sometimes it was out, and there'd be nothing but gold sand, and all the boats would be leaning on their sides."

"Didn't they fall over?"

"I don't think so."

"Why?"

"I haven't any idea," said Virginia.

There had been a special day, an April day of wind and sunshine. On that day the tide was high, Virginia could remember the salt smell of it, mixed with the evocative sea-going smells of tar and fresh paint.

Within the shelter of the quay the water swelled smooth and glassy, clear and deep. But beyond the harbour it was rough, the dark ocean flecked with white horses and, out across the bay, the great seas creamed against the rocks at the foot of the lighthouse, sending up spouts of white spray almost as high as the lighthouse itself.

It was a week since the night of the barbecue at Lanyon, and for once Virginia was on her own. Alice had driven to Penzance to attend some committee meeting, Tom Lingard was in Plymouth, Mrs. Jilkes, the cook, had her afternoon off and had departed, in a considerable hat to visit her cousin's wife, and Mrs. Parsons was keeping her weekly appointment with the hairdresser.

"You'll have to amuse yourself," she told Virginia over lunch.

"I'll be all right."

"What will you do?"

"I don't know. Something."

In the empty house, with the empty afternoon lying, like a gift, before her, she had considered a number of possibilities. But the marvellous day was too beautiful to be wasted, and she had gone out and started walking, and her feet had taken her down the narrow path that led to the cliffs, and then along the cliff path, and down to the white sickle of the beach. In the summer this would be crowded with coloured tents and ice-cream stalls and noisy holiday-makers with beach balls and umbrellas, but in April the visitors had not started to arrive, and the sand lay clean, washed by the winter storms, and her footsteps left a line of prints, neat and precise as little stitches.

At the far end, a lane leaned uphill and she was soon lost in a maze of narrow streets that wound between ancient, sun-bleached houses. She came upon flights of stone steps and unsuspected alleys and followed them down until all at once she turned a corner out at the very edge of the harbour. In a dazzle of sunshine she saw the bright-painted boats, the peacock-green water. Gulls screamed and wheeled overhead, their great wings like white sails against the blue, and everywhere there was activity and bustle, a regular spring-cleaning going on. Shopfronts were being white-washed, windows polished, ropes coiled, decks scrubbed, nets mended.

At the edge of the quay a hopeful vendor had set up his ice-cream barrow, shiny white, and lettered seductively "Fred Hoskings, Cornish Ice-cream, The Best Home-made" and Virginia suddenly longed for one, and wished she had brought some money. To sit in the sunshine on such a day and lick an ice-cream seemed, all at once, the height of luxury. The more she thought about it the more desirable it seemed, and she even went through all her pockets in the hope of finding some forgotten coin, but there was nothing there. Not so much as a half-penny.

She sat on a bollard and gazed disconsolately down on to the deck of a fishing boat where a young boy in a salt-stained smock was brewing up tea on a spirit lamp. She was trying not to think about the ice-cream when, like the answer to a prayer, a voice spoke from behind her.

"Hallo."

Virginia looked around over her shoulder, pushing her long dark hair out of her face, and saw him standing there, braced against the wind, with a package under his arm, and wearing a blue polo-necked sweater that made him look like a sailor.

She stood up. "Hallo."

"I thought it was you," said Eustace Philips, "but I couldn't be sure. What are you doing here?"

"Nothing. I mean, I just came for a walk, and I stopped to look at the boats."

"It's a lovely day."

"Yes."

His blue eyes gleamed, amused. "Where's Alice Lingard?"

"She's gone to Penzance . . . she's on a committee . . ."

"So you're all alone?"

"Yes." She was wearing worn blue sneakers, blue jeans and a white cable-stitch sweater, and felt miserably convinced that her naïvete was painfully obvious not only in her clothes but her lack of small-talk as well.

She looked at his package. "What are *you* doing here?"

"I came in to pick up a new rick cover. The wind last night blew the old one to ribbons."

"I expect you're going back now."

"Not immediately. How about you?"

"I'm not doing anything. Just exploring, I suppose."

"Don't you know the town?"

"I've never got this far before."

"Come along then, I'll show you the rest of it."

They began to walk back along the quay, in no hurry, their slow paces matched. He caught sight of the ice-cream barrow and stopped to talk.

"Hallo, Fred."

The ice-cream man, resplendent in a white starched coat like a cricket umpire, turned and saw him. A smile spread across features browned and wizened as a walnut.

" 'Allo, Eustace. 'Ow are you?"

"Fine. How's yourself?"

"Oh, keeping not too bad. Don't often see you down 'ere. 'Ow are things out at Lanyon?"

"All right. Working hard." Eustace ducked his head at the barrow. "You're early out. There's nobody here yet to buy ice-creams."

"Oh well, early bird catches the worm I always say."

Eustace looked at Virginia. "Do you want an ice-cream?"

She could not think of any person who had offered her, so instantly, exactly what she wanted most.

"I'd love one, but I haven't any money."

Eustace grinned. "The biggest you've got," he said to Fred, and reached his hand into the back pocket of his trousers.

He took her the length of the wharf, up cobbled streets at whose existence she had never even guessed, through small, surprising squares, where the houses had yellow doors and window-boxes, past little courtyards filled with washing-lines and flights of stone steps where the cats lay and sunned themselves and attended to their ablutions. They came out at last on to a northern beach which lay with its face to the wind, and the long combers rolled in jade green with the sun behind them, and the air was misted with blown spume.

"When I was a boy." Eustace told her, raising his voice above the wind, "I used to come here with a surf-board. A little wooden one my uncle made me, with a face painted on the curve. But now they have these Malibu surf-boards, made of fibreglass they are and they surf all year round, winter and summer."

"Isn't it cold?"

"They wear wet suits."

They came to a sea wall, curved against the wind with a wooden bench built into its angle and here Eustace, apparently deciding that they had walked far enough, settled himself, his back to the wall and his face to the sun and his long legs stretched in front of him.

Virginia, consuming the last of the mammoth ice-cream, sat beside him. He watched her, and when she had demolished the final mouthful and was wiping her fingers on the knees of her jeans he said, "Did you enjoy it?"

His face was serious but his eyes laughed at her. She didn't mind. "It was delicious. The best. You should have had one too."

"I'm too big and too old to go walking round the streets licking an ice-cream."

"I shall never be too big or too old."

"How old are you?"

"Seventeen, nearly eighteen."

"Have you left school?"

"Yes, last summer."

"What are you doing now?"

"Nothing."

"Are you going to University?"

65

She was flattered that he should imagine she was so clever. "Goodness, no."

"What are you going to do, then?"

Virginia wished that he had not asked.

"Well, eventually, I suppose, next winter I'll learn how to cook or do shorthand and typing or something gruesome like that. But you see my mother has this bee in her bonnet about being in London for the summer and going to all the parties and meeting all the right people and generally having a social whirl."

"I believe," said Eustace, "it's called 'Doing the Season.'"

His tone of voice made it very clear that he thought as little of the idea as she did.

"Oh, don't. It gives me the shivers."

"It's hard to believe, in this day and age, that anybody bothers any more."

"I know, it's fantastic. But they do. And my mother's one of them. She's already met some of the other mothers and had ghastly tea parties with them. She's even booked a date for a dance, but I'm going to try my hardest to talk her out of that one. Can you think of anything worse than having a coming-out dance?"

"No, I can't, but then I'm not a sweet seventeen-year-old." Virginia made a face at him. "If you feel so strongly about it why don't you dig in your toes, tell your mother you'd rather have the price of a return ticket to Australia or something?"

"I already have. At least I've tried. But you don't know my mother. She never listens to anything I say, she just says that it's so *important* to meet all the right people, and be asked to all the right parties and be seen at all the right places."

"You could try getting your father on your side."

"I haven't got a father. At least I never see him; they were divorced when I was a baby."

"I see." He added, without much heart: "Well, cheer up—who knows—you might enjoy it."

"I shall hate every moment of it."

"How do you know?"

"Because I'm useless at parties, and I get tongue-tied with strangers, and I can never think of anything to say to young men."

"You're thinking of plenty to say to me," Eustace pointed out.

"But you're different."

"How am I different?"

"Well, you're older. I mean you're not young." Eustace began to laugh and Virginia was embarrassed. "I mean you're not really young, like twenty-one or twenty-two." He was still laughing. She frowned. "How old *are* you?"

"Twenty-eight," he told her. "Twenty-nine next birthday."

"You are lucky. I wish I was twenty-eight."

"If you were," said Eustace, "you probably wouldn't be here now."

All at once it turned dark and cold. Virginia shivered, and looked up and saw that the sun had disappeared behind a large grey cloud, the vanguard of a bank of dirty weather which was blowing in from the west.

"That's it," said Eustace. "We've had the best of the day. It'll be raining by this evening." He looked at his watch. "It's nearly four o'clock, time I made for home. How are you getting back?"

"Walking, I suppose."

"Do you want a ride?"

"Have you got a car?"

"I've got a Land-Rover, parked round by the church."

"Won't I be taking you out of your way?"

"No. I can go back to Lanyon over the moor."

"Well, if you're certain . . ."

Driving back to Wheal House, Virginia fell silent. But it was a natural, companionable silence, comfortable as an old shoe, and had nothing to do with being shy or unable to think of anything to say. She could not remember when she had felt so at ease with a person—and certainly never with a man whom she had known such a short time. The Land-Rover was an old one, the seats worn and dusty and there were stray scraps of straw lying about the floor and a faint smell of farmyard manure. Virginia did not find this in the least offensive—rather, she liked it because it was part of Penfolda.

She realized that she wanted, above all things, to go back there. To see the farm and the fields in daylight, to inspect the stock and be shown around, perhaps to be allowed to see the rest of the farmhouse and be asked to tea in that enviable kitchen. To be accepted.

They came up the hill out of the town, where the houses of the old residential area had all been turned into hotels, with gardens bull-dozed into car parks, and glassed-in porches. There were sun-rooms and palm trees, dismal against the grey sky, and municipal flower-beds planted with straight rows of daffodils.

High above the sea, the road levelled out. Eustace changed into top gear and said, "When are you going back to London?"

"I don't know. In about a week."

"Do you want to come out to Penfolda again?"

This was the second time that day that he had offered her what she craved most. She wondered if he were psychic.

"Yes, I'd love to."

"My mother was very taken with you. Not often she sees a new face. It would be nice for her if you'd come and have a cup of tea with her."

"I'd like to come."

"How would you get out to Lanyon?" asked Eustace, his eyes on the road ahead.

"I could borrow Alice's car. I'm sure if I asked her she'd let me borrow it. I'd be very careful."

"Can you drive?"

"Of course. Otherwise I wouldn't borrow the car." She smiled at him. Not because it was meant to be a joke, but because all at once she felt so good.

"Well, I'll tell you," said Eustace in his deliberate way. "I'll have a word with my mother, find out which day suits her best, give you a ring on the telephone. How would that be?"

She imagined waiting for the call, having it come, hearing his voice over the wire. She almost hugged herself with pleasure.

"It would be all right."

"What's the number?"

"Porthkerris three two five."

"I'll remember that."

They had reached home. He turned into the white gates of Wheal House and roared up the drive between the hedges of escallonia.

"There you are!" He stopped with a great jerk of brakes and a splattering of gravel. "Home safely, just in time for tea."

"Thank you so much."

He leaned on the wheel, smiling at her. "That's all right."

"I mean, for everything. The ice-cream and everything."

"You're welcome." He reached across and opened the door for her. Virginia jumped down on to the gravel, and as she did so, the front door opened and Mrs. Parsons emerged, wearing a little suit of rasp-berry-red wool, and a white silk shirt, tied like a stock at the neck.

"Virginia!"

Virginia swung around. Her mother came across the gravel to-wards them, immaculate as always, but her hair, short and dark, blew casually in the wind and had obviously not been attended to that after-noon.

"Mother!"

"Where have you been?" The smile was friendly and interested. "I thought you were at the hairdresser."

"The girl who usually does me is in bed with a cold. They offered me another girl of course, but, as she's the one who usually spends her days sweeping hair off the floor, I declined with thanks." Still smiling, she looked beyond Virginia to where Eustace waited. "And who is your friend?"

"Oh. It's Eustace Philips . . ."

But now Eustace had decided to get out of the car. He jumped down on to the gravel and came around the front of the Land-Rover to be introduced. And, hating herself, Virginia saw him through her mother's eyes; the wide powerful shoulders beneath the sailor's sweater, the sun-burned face, the strong, calloused hands.

Mrs. Parsons came forward graciously. "How do you do."

"Hallo," said Eustace, meeting her eye with an unblinking blue gaze. Her hand was half-way out to shake his, but Eustace either didn't see this or chose to ignore it. Mrs. Parsons's hand dropped back to her side. Her manner became, subtly, a fraction more cool.

"Where did Virginia meet *you*?" The question was harmless, even playful.

Eustace leaned against the Land-Rover and crossed his arms. "I live out at Lanyon; farm Penfolda . . ."

"Oh, of course, the barbecue. Yes, I heard all about it. And how nice that you met up again today."

"By chance," said Eustace, firmly.

"But that makes it even nicer!" She smiled. "We're just going to have tea, Mr. Philips. Won't you join us?"

Eustace shook his head. His eyes never left her face. "I've got seventy cows waiting to be milked. I'd better be getting back . . ."

"Oh, of course. I wouldn't want to keep you from your work."

Her tone was that of the lady of the house dismissing the gardener, but she continued to smile.

"I wouldn't let you," said Eustace, and went to get back into the car.

"Goodbye, Virginia."

"Oh. Goodbye," said Virginia faintly. "And thank you for bringing me home."

"I'll ring you up some time."

"Yes, do that."

He gave a final salute with his head, then started the engine, put the Land-Rover into gear, and without a backward glance, shot away, down the drive and out of sight, leaving Virginia and her mother standing, staring after him, in a cloud of dust.

"Well!" said Mrs. Parsons, laughing, but obviously nettled.

Virginia said nothing. There did not seem to be anything to say.

"What a very basic young man! I must say, staying down here, one does meet all types. What's he going to ring you up about?"

The tone of her voice implied that Eustace Philips was something of a joke, a joke that she and Virginia shared.

"He thought perhaps I might go out to Lanyon and have tea with his mother."

"Isn't that marvellous? Pure Cold Comfort Farm." It began, very lightly, to rain. Mrs. Parsons glanced at the lowering sky and shivered. "What are we doing, standing out here in the wind? Come along, tea's waiting . . ."

Virginia thought nothing of the shiver, but the next morning her mother complained of feeling unwell, she had a cold, she said, an upset stomach, she would stay indoors. As the weather was horrible nobody questioned this, and Alice laid and lit a cheerful fire in the drawing-room, and by this Mrs. Parsons reclined on the sofa, a light mohair rug over her knees.

"I shall be perfectly all right," she told Virginia, "and you and Alice must just go off and not bother about me at all."

"What do you mean, we must just go off? Where is there to go off to?"

"To Falmouth. To lunch at Pendrane." Virginia stared blankly. "Oh, darling, don't look so gormless, Mrs. Menheniot asked us ages ago. She wanted to show us the garden."

"Nobody ever told me," said Virginia, who did not want to go. It would take all day to get to Falmouth and back again and have lunch and see the boring garden. She wanted to stay here and sit by the telephone and wait for Eustace to ring.

"Well, I'm telling you now. You'll have to change. You can't go out for lunch dressed in jeans. Why not wear that pretty blue shirt I bought for you? Or the tartan kilt? I'm sure Mrs. Menheniot would be amused by your kilt."

If she had been any other sort of a mother Virginia would have asked her to listen for the telephone, to take a message. But her mother did not like Eustace. She thought him ill-mannered and uncouth, and her smiling reference to Cold Comfort Farm had put the official stamp of disapproval upon him. Since his departure his name had not been mentioned, and although, during dinner last night, Virginia had tried more than once to tell Alice and Tom about her chance encounter, her mother had always firmly overridden the conversation, interrupting if necessary, and steering it into more suitable channels. While she changed, Virginia debated what to do.

Eventually, dressed in the kilt and a canary yellow sweater, with her dark hair brushed clean and shining, she went along to the kitchen to find Mrs. Jilkes. Mrs. Jilkes was a new friend. One wet afternoon she had taught Virginia to make scones, at the same time regaling her with a great deal of gratuitous information concerning the health and longevity of Mrs. Jilkes's numerous relations.

" 'Allo, Virginia."

She was rolling pastry. Virginia took a scrap and began, absently, to eat it.

"Now, don't go eating that! You'll fill yourself up, won't have no room for your lunch."

"I wish I didn't have to go. Mrs. Jilkes, if a phone call comes through for me, would you take a message?"

Mrs. Jilkes looked coy, rolling her eyes. "Expecting a phone call are you? Some young man, is it?"

Virginia blushed. "Well, all right, yes. But you will listen, won't you?"

"Don't you worry, my love. Now, there's Mrs. Lingard calling . . . time you was off. And I'll keep an eye on your mother, and give her a little lunch on a tray."

They did not return home until half past five. Alice went at once to the drawing-room, to inquire for Rowena Parsons's health, and to tell her all that they had done and seen. Virginia had made for the stairs, but the instant the drawing-room door was safely closed, turned and sprinted down the kitchen passage.

"Mrs. Jilkes!"

"Back again, are you?"

"Was there a phone call?"

"Yes, two or three, but your mother answered them."

"Mother?"

"Yes, she had the phone switched through to the drawing-room. You'll have to ask her if there are any messages."

Virginia went out of the kitchen, and back down the passage, across the hall and into the drawing-room. Across Alice Lingard's head, her eyes met and held her mother's cool gaze. Then Mrs. Parsons smiled.

"Darling! I've been hearing all about it. Was it fun?"

"It was all right." She waited, giving her mother the chance to tell her that the telephone call had come through.

"All right? No more? I believe Mrs. Menheniot's nephew was there?"

". . . Yes."

Already the image of the chinless young man was so blurred that she could scarcely remember his face. Perhaps Eustace would ring tomorrow. He couldn't have phoned today. Virginia knew her mother. Knew that, however much she disapproved, Mrs. Parsons would be meticulous about such social obligations as passing on telephone messages. Mothers were like that. They had to be. Because if they didn't live by the code of behaviour which they preached, then they lost all right to their children's trust. And without trust there could be no affection. And without affection, nothing.

The next day it rained. All morning, Virginia sat by the fire in the hall, pretending to read a book, and flying to answer the telephone each time it rang. It was never for her; it was never Eustace.

After lunch her mother asked her to go down to the chemist in Porthkerris to pick up a prescription. Virginia said she didn't want to go.

". . . It's pouring with rain."

"A little rain won't hurt you. Besides, the exercise will do you good. You've been sitting indoors all day, reading that silly book."

"It's not a silly book . . ."

"Well, anyway, reading. Put on some wellingtons and a raincoat and you won't even notice the rain . . ."

It was no good arguing. Virginia made a resigned face and went to find her raincoat. Trudging down the road towards the town, the pavements dark and grey between the dripping trees, she tried to face up to the unthinkable possibility that Eustace was never going to ring her.

He had said that he would, certainly, but it all seemed to depend on what his mother said, when she would be free, when Virginia would be able to borrow the car and drive herself out to Lanyon.

Perhaps Mrs. Philips had changed her mind. Perhaps she had said, "Oh Eustace, I haven't got time for tea parties . . . what were you thinking of, saying she could come out here?"

Perhaps, having met Virginia's mother, Eustace had changed his own mind about Virginia. They said that if you wanted to know what sort of a wife a girl was going to turn into, you looked at her mother. Perhaps Eustace had looked and decided that he did not like what he saw. She remembered the challenge in his unblinking blue eyes, and that final bitter exchange.

"I wouldn't want to keep you from your work."

"I wouldn't let you."

Perhaps he had forgotten to telephone. Perhaps he had had second thoughts. Or perhaps—and this was chilling—Virginia had misconstrued his friendliness, unburdened all her problems, and so aroused his sympathy. Perhaps that was all it was. That he was sorry for her.

But he said he would telephone. He said he would.

She collected the prescription and started home once more. It was still raining. Across the street from the chemist stood a call-box. It was empty. It would all be so simple. It wouldn't take a moment to look up his number, to dial. She had her purse in her pocket, with coins to pay for the call. *It's Virginia*, she would say, and make a joke of it, teasing him. *I thought you were going to ring me up!*

She almost crossed the road. At the edge of the pavement she hesitated, trying to pluck up the courage to take the initiative in a situation which was beyond her.

She imagined the conversation.

"Eustace?"

"Yes."

"This is Virginia."

"Virginia?"

"Virginia Parsons."

"Oh, yes. Virginia Parsons. What do you want?"

But at this point her courage turned on its heels and fled, and Virginia never crossed the road to the telephone box, but carried on up the hill with the rain in her face and her mother's pills deep in the pocket of her waterproof coat.

As she came in through the front door of Wheal House she heard the telephone ringing, but by the time she had got her wellingtons off the ringing had stopped, and by the time she burst into the drawing-room, her mother was just putting down the receiver.

She raised her eyebrows at her breathless daughter.

"Whatever's wrong?"

"I . . . I thought it might be for me."

"No. A wrong number. Did you get my pills, darling?"

"Yes," said Virginia dully.

"Sweet of you. And the walk has done you good. I can tell. Your cheeks are quite pink again."

The next day Mrs. Parsons announced out of the blue that they must return to London. Alice was astonished. "But, Rowena, I thought you were going to stay at least another week."

"Darling, we'd love to, but you know, we do have a very busy summer to put in, and a lot of arrangements and organization to be seen to. I don't think we can sit here enjoying ourselves for another week. Much as I would adore to."

"Well, anyway, stay over the week-end."

Yes, stay over the week-end, Virginia prayed. *Please, please, please stay over the week-end.*

But it wasn't any use. "Oh, adore to, but we must go . . . Friday at the latest I'm afraid. I'll have to see about booking seats on the train."

"Well, it seems a shame, but if you really mean it . . ."

"Yes, darling, I really do mean it."

Let him remember. Let him phone. There wouldn't be time to go out to Penfolda but at least I could say goodbye, I'd know that he'd meant it . . . perhaps I could say I'd write to him, perhaps I could give him my address.

"Darling, I wish you'd get on with your packing. Don't leave anything behind, it would be such a bore for poor Alice to have to parcel it up. Have you put your raincoat in?"

This evening. He'll ring this evening. He'll say, I am sorry but I've been away; I've been so busy I haven't had a moment; I've been ill.

"Virginia! Come and write your name in the visitors' book! There, under mine. Oh, Alice, my dear, what a wonderful holiday you've given us. Sheer delight. We've both adored it, haven't we, Virginia? Can't bear to go."

They went. Alice drove them to the station, saw them into their first-class carriage, the corner seats reserved, the porter being deferential because of Mrs. Parsons's expensive luggage.

"You'll come again soon," said Alice as Virginia leaned out of the window to kiss her.

"Yes."

"We've loved having you . . ."

It was the last chance. *Tell Eustace I had to go. Tell him goodbye for me.* The whistle shrilled, the train began to move. *Ring him up when you get back.*

"Goodbye, Virginia."

Send him my love. Tell him I love him.

By Truro her misery had become so obvious with sniffs and sobs and brimming tears that her mother could ignore them no longer.

"Oh, darling." She put down her newspaper. "Whatever is the matter?"

"Nothing . . ." Virginia stood at the window swollen-faced, unseeing.

"But it has to be something." She put out a hand and put it, gently, on Virginia's knee. "Was it that young man?"

"Which young man?"

"The young man in the Land-Rover, Eustace Philips? Did you break your heart over him?" Virginia, weeping, could make no reply. Her mother went on, reassuring, gentle. "I wouldn't be too unhappy. It's probably the first time you've been hurt by a man, but I assure you it won't be the last. They're selfish creatures, you know."

"Eustace wasn't like that."

"Wasn't he?"

"He was kind. He was the only man I've ever really liked." She blew her nose lustily and gazed at her mother. "You didn't like him, did you?"

Mrs. Parsons was momentarily taken aback by such unusual directness. "Well . . . let's say I've never been very fond of his type."

"You mean, you didn't like him being a farmer?"

"I never said that."

"No, but that's what you mean. You only like chinless weeds like Mrs. Menheniot's nephew."

"I never met Mrs. Menheniot's nephew."

"No. But you would have liked him."

Mrs. Parsons did not reply to this at once. But after a little she said, "Forget him, Virginia. Every girl has to have one unhappy love affair before she finally meets the right man and settles down and gets married. And this summer's going to be such fun for us both. It would be a pity to spoil it, yearning for something that probably never even existed."

"Yes," said Virginia and wiped her eyes and put her sodden handkerchief away in her pocket.

"That's a good girl. Now, no more tears." And, satisfied that she had poured oil on troubled waters, Mrs. Parsons sat back in her seat and picked up the newspaper again. But presently, disquieted, disturbed by something, she lowered the paper and saw that Virginia was watching her, unblinking, an expression in her dark eyes that her mother had never seen before.

"What is it?"

Virginia said, "He said he'd phone. He promised he'd telephone me."

"Well?"

"Did he? You didn't like him, I know. Did you take the call and never tell me?"

Her mother never hesitated. "Darling! What an accusation. Of course not. You surely didn't think . . . ?"

"No," said Virginia dully as the last flicker of hope died. "No, I never thought." And she turned to lean her forehead against the smeared glass of the train window, and the rocketing countryside, together with everything else that had happened, streamed away, for ever, into the past.

That was April. In May Virginia met up again with an old schoolfriend, who invited her down to the country for the week-end.

"It's my birthday, darling, too super, Mummy says I can ask anyone I like, you'll probably have to sleep in the attic, but you won't mind, will you? We're such a madly disorganized family."

Virginia, taking all this with a pinch of salt, accepted the invitation. "How do I get there?"

"Well, you *could* catch a train, and someone *could* meet you, but that's so dreadfully boring. I tell you what, my cousin's probably coming, he's got a car, he'll maybe give me a lift. I'll speak to him and see if he's got room for you. You'll probably have to squeeze in with the luggage or sit on the gear lever, but anything's better than fighting the crowds at Waterloo . . ."

Rather surprisingly, she duly arranged this. The car was a dark blue Mercedes coupé, and once Virginia's luggage had been crammed into the over-loaded boot, she was invited to squash herself into the front seat, between the girl-friend and the cousin. The cousin was tall and fair, with long legs and a grey suit and hair that curled in ducks' tails from beneath the brim of his forward-tilted brown trilby hat.

His name was Anthony Keile.

Chapter 6

TRAVEL-WORN AND TIRED, and with all the problems of Bosithick still to be faced, Virginia got out of the train at Penzance, took a lungful of cool sea air, and was thankful to be back. The tide was low, the air strong with the smell of seaweed. Across the bay, St. Michael's Mount stood gold in the evening sun, and the wet sands were streaked with blue, where small streams and shallow pools of sea-water gave back the colour of the sky.

Miraculously, here was a porter. As they followed him and his barrow out of the station Nicholas said, "Is this where we're going to stay?"

"No, we've got to drive over to Lanyon."

"How are we going to drive?"

"I told you, I left my car here."

"How do you know it hasn't been stolen?"

"Because I can see it, waiting for us."

It took some time to pack all their belongings into the boot of the Triumph. But in the end it was all piled in, crowned by the cardboard crate of groceries, and Virginia tipped the porter and they got in, all three of them in the front seat, with Cara in the middle, and the door on Nicholas's side firmly locked.

She had put down the hood and then tied a scarf around her head, but the wind blew Cara's hair forward all over her face.

"How long will it take us to get there?"

"Not long, about half an hour."

"What does the house look like?"

"Why don't you wait and see?"

78

At the top of the hill she stopped the car, and they looked back to see the view, the lovely curve of Mount's Bay, still and blue, enclosed in the warmth of the day that was over. And all about them were little fields, and ditches blue with wild scabious, and they went on and dropped into a miniature valley filled with ancient oak trees, and a stream ran beneath a bridge, and there was an old mill and a village, and then the road twined up on to the moor again, and all at once the straight bright horizon of the Atlantic lay before them, glittering to the westward in a dazzle of sun.

"I thought the sea was behind us," said Nicholas. "Is that another sea?"

"I suppose it is."

"Is that our sea? Is that the one we're going to use?"

"I expect so."

"Is there a beach?"

"I haven't had time to look. There are certainly a lot of steep cliffs."

"I want a beach. With sand. I want you to buy me a bucket and spade."

"All in good time," said Virginia. "How about taking things one at a time?"

"I want to buy a bucket and spade *tomorrow*."

They joined the main road and turned east, running parallel to the coast. They left Lanyon village behind them and the road which led to Penfolda, and they climbed the hill and came to the clump of leaning hawthorns which marked the turning to Bosithick.

"Here we are!"

"But there's no house."

"You'll see."

Bumped and jarred, the car and its occupants lurched down the lane. From beneath them came sinister banging sounds, the great gorse bushes closed in at either side, and Cara, anxious for their provisions, reached back a hand to hang on to the grocery carton. They swung around the last corner with a final lurch, ran up on to the grass bank at a frightening angle, and stopped with a jerk. Virginia put on the hand-brake, turned off the engine. And the children sat in the car and stared at the house.

In Penzance there had been no wind, the air was milky and breathlessly warm. Here, there was a faint whining, a coolness. The broken washing line stirred in the breeze and the long grass at the top of the stone hedge lay flattened like a fur coat, stroked by a hand.

And there was something else. Something was wrong. For a moment Virginia stared, trying to think what it was. And then Cara told her. "There's smoke in the chimney," said Cara.

Virginia shivered, a frisson of unease, like a trickle of cold water ran down her spine. It was as though they had caught the house unawares, they had not been expected by the nameless, unimagined beings who normally occupied it.

Cara felt her disquiet. "Is anything wrong?"

"No, of course not." She sounded more robust than she felt. "I was just surprised. Let's go and investigate."

They got out of the car, leaving the cases and groceries behind. Virginia manhandled the gate open and stood aside for the children to go through while she felt in her bag for the ring of keys.

They went ahead of her, Nicholas running, to investigate what lay around the far corner of the house, but Cara trod cautiously as though trespassing, avoiding an old rag, a broken flower-pot, her hands held fastidiously, anxious not to be asked to touch anything.

Together, they opened the front door. As it swung inwards Cara said, "Do you suppose it's Gipsies?"

"What's Gipsies?"

"Who've lit the fire."

"Let's look . . ." The smell of mice and damp had gone. Instead the house felt fresh and warm, and when they stepped into the living-room they found it bright with firelight. The whole aspect of the house was changed by this, it was sullen and depressing no longer . . . on the contrary, quite cheerful. The hideous electric fire had somehow been disposed of, and a tall rush basket stood by the hearth, piled with a good supply of logs.

What with the fire and the last of the afternoon sun filtering in through the west window, the room was very warm. Virginia went to open a window, and saw, through the open kitchen door, the bowl set on the table, piled with brown eggs, the white enamel milk pan. She went into the kitchen and stood in the middle of the floor and stared. Someone had been in and cleaned the place up, the sink was shining and the curtains laundered.

Cara stole in behind her, still cautious. "It's like fairies," she said.

"It's not fairies," said Virginia, smiling. "It's Alice."

"Aunt Alice Lingard?"

"Yes, isn't she a dear? She pretended to be so disapproving about us coming to Bosithick and then she goes and does a thing like this. But that's just like Alice. She's very kind. We'll have to go tomorrow and thank her. I'd ring up, only we haven't got a telephone."

"I hate the telephone anyway. And I want to go and see her. I want to see the swimming pool."

"If you take your bathing-suit you can have a swim."

Cara stood staring up at her mother. Virginia thought she was still thinking about swimming and was surprised when she said, "How did she get in?"

"Who?"

"Aunt Alice. We've got the keys."

"Oh. Well. I expect she got a spare key from Mr. Williams. Something like that. Now what are we going to do first?"

Nicholas appeared at the door. "I'm going to look all over the house and then I want some tea. I'm starving!"

"Take Cara with you."

"I want to stay with *you*."

"No." Virginia gave her a gentle push. "You go and tell me what you think of the rest of the house. Tell me if you don't think it the funniest house you've ever seen in your life. And I'll put the kettle on and we'll boil some eggs, and after that we'll bring all the stuff in from the car and see about unpacking and making the beds."

"Aren't the beds even made?"

"No, we've got to do it all. We're really on our own now."

Somehow, by the end of the evening they had managed to attain a semblance of order, but finding the switch for the hot-water tank and the cupboard where the sheets were kept, and trying to decide who was going to sleep in which bed, all took a very long time. For supper Nicholas wanted baked beans on toast, but they couldn't find a toaster and the grill on the cooker was fiercely temperamental, so he had baked beans on bread instead.

"We need washing-up stuff and a mop, and tea and coffee . . ." Virginia searched for a piece of paper and a pencil and started, frantically, to make a list.

Cara chimed in, ". . . And soap for the bathroom and stuff to clean the bath with, because it's got a *horrid* dirty mark."

"And a bucket and spade," said Nicholas.

"And we'll have to get a fridge," said Cara. "We haven't got any-where to keep our food and it'll all grow a blue beard if we let it just lie about."

Virginia said, "Perhaps we could borrow a meat-safe," and then remembered who had offered to lend her one, and frowned down at her shopping list and hastily changed the subject.

When the little water tank finally heated up, they had baths in the gimcrack bathroom, Nicholas and Cara going in together, and then Virginia swiftly before the water went cold. In dressing-gowns, by fire-light, they made cocoa . . .

"There isn't even a television."

"Or a wireless."

"Or a clock," said Nicholas cheerfully.

Virginia smiled and looked at her watch. "If you really want to know, it's ten past nine."

"Ten past nine! We should be in bed ages ago."

"It doesn't matter," she told them.

"Doesn't *matter*? Nanny would be furious!"

Virginia leaned back in her chair, stretched out her legs and wrig-gled her bare toes at the heat of the fire.

"I know," she said.

After they were in bed, after she had kissed them, and left the door open on the landing and showed them how the light worked, she left them, and went down the narrow passage and up the two steps that led to the Tower Room.

It was cold. She sat by the window and looked out across the still, shadowed fields, and saw that the peaceful sea had turned pearly in the dusk, and the sky in the afterglow of sunset was streaked in long scarves of coral. Clouds were gathered in the west. They lay, piled beyond the horizon, threaded with shafts of gold and pink light, but gradually even these last shreds of light filtered away, and the clouds turned black, and in the east a little new moon, like an eyelash, floated up into the sky.

One by one lights started to twinkle out across the soft darkness, along the whole length of the coast, from farm-houses, and cottages and barns. Here, a window burned square and yellow. There a light bobbed across a rick yard. A pair of headlights tunnelled up a lane, and headed out on to the main road towards Lanyon, and Virginia won-dered if it was Eustace Philips, making for Lanyon and The Mermaid's

Arms, and she wondered if he would come and see how they were getting along, or whether he would be taciturn and sulky and wait for Virginia to produce some sort of an olive branch. She told herself that it would be worth doing even this, if it were only for the satisfaction of seeing his face when he realized how well she and Cara and Nicholas were managing for themselves.

But next day it was different.

In the night the wind had got up, and the dark clouds which last evening had lain banked on the horizon, were blown inland, bringing with them a dark and drenching rain. The sound of gutters trickling and dripping, the rattle of raindrops against the glass of the window-pane were the sounds which woke Virginia up. Her bedroom was so gloomy that she had to turn on the lamp before she could read her watch. Eight o'clock.

She got of bed and went and shut the window. The floor-boards beneath her feet were quite wet. The rain curtained everything, and she could see no more than a few yards. It was like being in a ship, marooned in a sea of rain. She hoped the children would not wake up for hours.

She dressed in trousers and her thickest jersey and went downstairs and found that the rain had come down the chimney and effectively put out the fire, and the room felt damp and chilly. There were matches, but no firelighters; wood, but no kindling. She pulled on a raincoat and went out into the rain and across to the sagging garden shed, and found a hatchet, blunt with age and misuse. On the stone front doorstep, and at considerable personal danger to herself, she chopped a log into kindling, then took some paper which had been wrapped in with their groceries, and kindled a little fire. The sticks snapped and crackled, the smoke, after one or two surly billows into the room, ran sweetly up the chimney. She piled on logs and left the fire to burn.

Cara appeared when she was cooking breakfast.

"Mummy!"

"Hallo, my love." She bent to kiss her. Cara wore sky blue shorts, a yellow tee shirt, an inadequate little cardigan. "Are you warm enough?"

"No," said Cara. Her fine, straight hair was bunched into a slide, her spectacles were crooked. Virginia straightened them. "Go and put on some more clothes, then. Breakfast isn't ready yet."

"But there isn't anything else. In my suitcase, I mean. Nanny didn't pack anything else."

"I don't believe it!" They gazed at each other. "You mean no jeans or raincoats or gum-boots."

Cara shook her head. "I suppose she thought it was going to be hot."

"Yes, I suppose she did," said Virginia mildly, mentally cursing Nanny. "But you'd have thought she knew enough about packing to put a raincoat in."

"Well, we've sort of got raincoats, but not proper ones."

She looked so worried that Virginia smiled. "Don't worry."

"What shall we do?"

"We'll have to go and buy you both some clothes."

"Today?"

"Why not? We can't do anything else in weather like this."

"How about seeing Aunt Alice and swimming in her pool?"

"We'll keep that for a finer day. She won't mind. She'll understand."

They drove through the downpour to Penzance. At the top of the hill the mist was thick and grey, swirling in the wind, parting momentarily to allow a glimpse of the road ahead, and then closing in once more so that Virginia could scarcely see the end of the bonnet.

Penzance was awash with rain, traffic and disconsolate holiday-makers, prevented by the weather from their usual daily ploy of sitting on the promenade or the beach. They clogged the pavements, stood in shop doorways, aimlessly surged round the counters of shops, looking for something to buy. Behind the steamy windows of cafés and ice-cream shops they could be seen, packed in at little tables, slowly sipping, licking, munching; spinning it out, making it last, so that as to postpone the inevitable moment when they had to go out into the rain again.

Virginia drove around for ten minutes before she found a place to leave the car. In the rain they searched the choked streets until they came to a shop where fishermen's oilskins were for sale, and huge thigh-length rubber boots and lanterns and rope, and they went in and she bought jeans for Cara and Nicholas, and dark blue Guernseys, and black oilskins and sou'westers which obliterated the children like candle-snuffers. The children put on the new oilskins and the sou'westers, then and there, but the rest of the clothes were tied up in a brown paper parcel. Virginia took the parcel and paid the bill, and with the children, stiff as robots in their new coats, blinded by the brims of the hats, she went out into the street again.

It still poured. "Let's go home now," said Cara.

"Well, while we're here, we may as well get some fish or some meat or a chicken. And we haven't any potatoes or carrots or peas. There may be a supermarket."

"I want a bucket and spade," said Nicholas.

Virginia pretended not to hear. They found the supermarket, and joined the herd-like crowds, queuing and choosing, waiting and paying, packing the parcels into carriers, lugging them out of the shop.

The gutters gurgled, water streamed from drainpipes.

"Cara, can you really carry that?"

"Yes . . ." said Cara, dragged down to one side by the weight of the carrier.

"Give half of it to Nicholas."

"I want a bucket and spade," said Nicholas.

But Virginia had run out of money. She was about to tell him that he would have to wait until the next shopping expedition, but he turned up his face under the brim of the sou'wester, and his mouth was mutinous, but his eyes huge and beginning to brim with tears. "I want a bucket and spade."

"Well, we'll buy you one. But first I'll have to find a bank and cash a cheque and get more money."

The tears, as if by magic, vanished. "I saw a bank!"

They found the bank, filled with queuing customers.

The children made their way to a leather bench and sat, exhausted, like two little old people, their chins sunk into their chests, and their legs stuck out in front of them, regardless of whom they might trip up. Virginia waited in a queue, then produced her bank card and wrote her cheque.

"On holiday?" asked the young cashier. Virginia wondered how he could still be good-tempered at the end of such a morning.

"Yes."

"It'll clear up by tomorrow, you'll see."

"I hope so."

The red bucket and the blue spade was their final purchase. Laden, they walked the long way back to the car, and for some reason it was all uphill. Nicholas, banging the bucket with the spade as though it were a drum, trailed behind. More than once Virginia had to turn and wait for him, exhort him to get a move on. Finally, she lost her patience. "Oh, Nicholas, *do* hurry," and a passing woman heard the suppressed irritation in her voice, and glanced back, her face full of disapproval at such a disagreeable and short-tempered mother.

And that was after only one morning.

It still rained. They came at last to the car, and loaded the boot with parcels, and pulled off their dripping raincoats and stuffed them into the boot, and then scrambled into the car and slammed the door, thankful beyond words to be at last sitting down and out of the rain.

"Now," said Nicholas, still banging the bucket with the spade, "do you know what I want?"

Virginia looked at her watch. It was nearly one o'clock. "Something to eat?" she guessed.

What I would like would be to go back to Wheal House and know that Mrs. Jilkes had lunch ready and waiting, and there would be a cheerful fire in the drawing-room, and lots of new magazines and newspapers and nothing to do for the rest of the afternoon except read them.

"Yes, that. But something else as well."

"I don't know."

"You've got to guess. I'll give you three guesses."

"Well." She thought. "You want to go to the loo?"

"No. At least not yet."

"You want . . . a drink of water?"

"No."

"Give in."

"I want to go to a beach this afternoon and dig. With my new bucket and spade."

The young man in the bank proved to be quite correct in his weather forecast. That evening, the wind swung around to the north, and the shredded clouds were sent bowling away, over the moors. At first small patches of sky appeared, and then these grew larger and brighter and at last the evening sun broke through, to set, triumphantly, in a welter of glorious pinks and reds.

"Red Sky At Night, Shepherd's Delight," said Cara as they went to bed. "That means it's going to be a lovely day tomorrow."

It was.

"I want to go to the beach today and dig with my bucket and spade," said Nicholas.

"You will," Virginia told him firmly. "But first we have to go and see Aunt Alice Lingard, otherwise she'll think we're the rudest, most ungrateful people she's ever known."

"Why?" said Nicholas.

"Because she got the house all ready for us and we haven't even said thank you . . . finish up your egg, Nicholas, it's getting all cold."

"I wish I could have cornflakes."

"We'll buy cornflakes," said Virginia, and Cara got the pencil and the shopping list and they wrote Cornflakes underneath Steel Wool, Peanut Butter and Caster Sugar, Splits, Jellies, Soap Powder and Cheese. Virginia had never done so much shopping in her life.

She sent them off to play while she did the breakfast dishes and went upstairs to make the beds. The children's room was awash with clothes. Virginia had always imagined they were neat and tidy, but realized now that it had simply been Nanny, who moved along behind them, picking up and putting away everything that they dropped. She gathered up the clothes, not knowing if they were dirty or clean, took a sock from the top of the chest of drawers, and carefully did not touch a crumpled paper bag with two sticky sweets in the corner.

There was also a big pigskin folder of photographs. This belonged to Cara, and had been packed by Nanny, with what intention Virginia could only guess. One side of the folder was taken up with a selection of small photographs, many of which had been taken by Cara herself, and arranged with more affection than artistry. The front of the house, rather crooked; the dogs, the farm men on the tractor; an aerial view of Kirkton, and a picture postcard or two. On the other side was an impressive studio portrait of Anthony, a head and shoulders, all lighting and angles, so that his hair looked white blond, and his jaw very square and determined. The photographer's impression was of a strong man, but Virginia knew the narrowed eyes, and the weak, handsome mouth. And she saw the striped collar of the Turnbull and Asher shirt, the discreetly patterned silk of the Italian tie, and she remembered how clothes had mattered to Anthony; just as his car was important, and the furnishings of his house and his manner of living. Virginia had always imagined that these were subsidiary considerations, and took their shape from the character of the individual. But with Anthony Keile it was the other way round, and he had invariably given the highest priority to the smallest details, as though realizing that they were the props behind his image, and without them his inadequate personality would crumble.

Carrying the armful of clothes, she went downstairs and washed them in the tiny sink. When she took these outside to peg them crookedly on to the knotted clothes-line, she found only Nicholas, alone, playing with his red tractor and a few pebbles and bits of grass. He wore his new navy-blue Guernsey and was already scarlet in the face with heat, but Virginia knew better than to suggest that it might be a good idea if he took the sweater off.

"What are you playing?"

"Nothing much . . ."

"Is the grass straw?"

"Sort of."

Virginia pegged out the last pair of pants. "Where's Cara?"

"She's inside."

"Reading, I expect," said Virginia and went in to find her. But Cara was not reading; she was in the Tower Room, sitting by the window staring sightlessly out across the fields to the sea. When Virginia appeared at the door, she turned her head slowly, bemused, unrecognizing.

"Cara . . ."

Her eyes behind the spectacles came into focus. She smiled. "Hallo. Is it time to go . . . ?"

"I'm ready when you are." She sat beside Cara. "What are you doing? Thinking, or looking at the view."

"Both, really."

"What were you thinking about?"

"I was really wondering how long we were going to stay here . . ."

"Oh—I suppose about a month. I've taken it for a month."

"But we'll have to go back to Scotland, won't we? We'll have to go back to Kirkton."

"Yes, we'll have to go back. There's your school for one thing." She waited. "Don't you want to go?"

"Isn't Nanny coming with us?"

"I shouldn't think so."

"It'll be funny, won't it, Kirkton, without Daddy or Nanny? It's so big for just the three of us. I think that's why I like this house. It's just the right size."

"I thought perhaps you wouldn't like it."

"I love it. And I love this room. I've never seen a room like it, with the stairs going down in the middle of the floor and all the windows and the sky." She was obviously not bothered by spooky sensations. "Why isn't there any furniture, though?"

"I think it was built as a study, a workroom. There was a man who lived here, about fifty years ago. He wrote books and he was very famous."

"What did he look like?"

"I don't know. I suppose he had a beard, and perhaps he was rather untidy and forgot to do up his sock suspenders, and buttoned his suit all wrong. Writers are often very absent-minded."

"What was his name?"

"Aubrey Crane."

"I'm sure he was nice," said Cara, "to have made such a pretty room. You can just sit and see everything that happens."

"Yes," said Virginia, and together they gazed out at the patchwork fields, where peaceful cows grazed, and the grass was emerald green after the rain, and stone walls and leaning gate posts were tangled with brambles which, in just a month or two, would be sweet and heavy with black fruit. Away to the west a tractor hummed. She turned her head, pressing her forehead against the window and saw the patch of scarlet, bright as a pillar-box, and the man sitting up behind the wheel, wearing a shirt as blue as the sky.

"Who's that?" asked Cara.

"That's Eustace Philips."

"Do you know him?"

"Yes. He farms Penfolda."

"Are these all his fields?"

"I expect so."

"When did you know him?"

"A long time ago."

"Does he know you're here?"

"Yes, I think so."

"I expect he'll come for a drink or something."

Virginia smiled. "Yes, perhaps he will. Now come and comb your hair and get ready. We're going to see Alice Lingard."

"Shall I put in my bathing things? Can we swim in her pool?"

"That's a good idea."

"I wish we had a swimming pool."

"What, here? There wouldn't be room in the garden."

"No, not here. At Kirkton."

"Well, we could," said Virginia, without thinking. "If you really wanted one. But do let's go, otherwise it'll be lunchtime, and we shall have done nothing but sit here and talk."

But when they got to Wheal House, they found only Mrs. Jilkes at home. Virginia had rung the bell but only as a formality, immediately opening the door and stepping into the hall with the children at her heels. She waited for the dog to start barking, for Alice's voice to say "Who is it" and Alice to appear through the drawing-room door. But she was met only by silence, broken by the slow ticking of the grandfather clock which stood by the fireplace.

"Alice?"

Somewhere a door opened and shut. And then Mrs. Jilkes came up the kitchen passage, like a ship in full sail with her starched white apron. "Who is it?" She sounded quite cross until she saw Virginia standing there with the children beside her.

Then she smiled. "Oh, Mrs. Keile, you did surprise me, I couldn't think who you were, standing there. And these are your children. My, aren't they lovely? Aren't you lovely?" she inquired conversationally of Cara, who had never been asked such a question before. She wondered if she would say "no" because she knew that she wasn't lovely, but she was too shy to say anything. She simply stared at Mrs. Jilkes.

"Cara, isn't it? And Nicholas. Brought your swimming things, too, I can see. Going to go and have a dip in the pond?" She turned back to Virginia. "Mrs. Lingard's not here."

"Oh dear."

"Been away she has, ever since you went. Mr. Lingard had to go to some big dinner in London, so Mrs. Lingard suddenly decided she'd go too. Said she hadn't been up for a bit. She'll be home this evening, though."

Virginia worked this out. "You mean, she's been away since Thursday?"

"Thursday afternoon she went."

"But . . . Bosithick . . . A fire had been lighted when we got there, and it was all clean and there were eggs and milk waiting for us . . . I thought it was Mrs. Lingard."

Mrs. Jilkes looked coy.

"No. But I'll tell you who it was, though."

"Who was it?"

"It was Eustace Philips."

"*Eustace?*"

"Well, don't sound so shocked, it's not as though he's done any-thing wrong."

"But how do you know it was Eustace?"

"Because he telephoned me," Mrs. Jilkes said, importantly. "Least, he telephoned Mrs. Lingard, but her being in London I spoke to him instead. And he said was anybody doing anything about you coming back to Bosithick with those children, and I said I didn't know, and told him Mrs. Lingard was away, and he said, 'Well, never mind, I'll look after it,' and that was it. Make a good job, did he?"

"You mean he came in and did all that *house-cleaning*?"

"Oh no. Eustace wouldn't know one end of a duster from the other. That would have been Mrs. Thomas. She'd scrub the flags off the floor if you'd give her half a chance."

Cara put her hand into Virginia's. "Is that the man on the tractor we saw this morning?"

"Yes," said Virginia, distracted.

"But won't he think we're terribly rude? We haven't said thank you."

"No, I know. We'll have to go this afternoon. When we get back, we'll go down to Penfolda and explain."

Nicholas was furious. "But you said I could dig on the beach with my bucket and spade!"

Mrs. Jilkes knew a rebellious voice when she heard one. She stooped towards Nicholas, hands on her knees, her face close to his, her voice seductive.

"Why don't you go and have a lovely swim? And when you come out you and your Mummy and your sister can come and eat shepherd's pie, in the kitchen with Mrs. Jilkes . . ."

"Oh, but Mrs. Jilkes . . ."

"*No.*" Mrs. Jilkes shook her head at Virginia's interruption. "It's no trouble. All waiting to be eaten it is. And I was just beginning to think that the house was somehow empty, and me rattling around in it like a pea in a drum." She beamed at Cara. "You'd like to do that, wouldn't you, my lovely?"

She was so kind that Cara's icy shyness thawed. She said, "Yes, please."

That warm Sunday afternoon they walked across the fields to Penfolda, across the stubble fields where, only a week ago, Virginia had watched the harvesters at work; across the grassy meadows, going from field to field by stiles made of granite steps laid across the open ditches. As they approached the farm, they saw the dutch barns, the gates, the concrete cattle court, the milking parlours. Cautiously opening and shutting the gates behind them they crossed the court and came out in the old cobbled farmyard. There was the sound of scrubbing, wet bristles on stone, and Virginia went to an open door of what looked like stables, with loose boxes, and found a man, who was not Eustace, cleaning the place out. He wore a faded navy-blue beret on the back of his curly grey head, and old-fashioned dungarees with braces.

He saw her and stopped sweeping. Virginia said, "I'm sorry, I'm looking for Mr. Philips . . ."

" 'E's around somewhere . . . up at the back of the house . . ."

"We'll see if we can find him."

They went through a gate, and along a path that led between the farmhouse and the tangled little garden where she and Eustace had shared the pasty. A tabby cat sat on the doorstep in a warm patch of sun. Cara squatted to pet it and Virginia knocked on the door. There were footsteps and the door opened, and a little round woman stood there, cosy as an arm-chair, upholstered in a black dress and loose-covered with a print apron. From behind her, from the kitchen, came a good smell, the memory of a hearty Sunday dinner.

"Yes?"

"I'm Virginia Keile . . . from Bosithick . . ."

"Oh *yes* . . ."

A smile creased the rosy face, pushing up her cheeks into two little bunches.

"You must be Mrs. Thomas."

"That's right . . . and these your children, are they?"

"Yes. Cara and Nicholas. We feel so bad because we never came down to thank you. For cleaning the house I mean, and leaving the eggs and the milk and the firewood and everything."

"Oh, that wasn't me. I just cleaned the place up a bit, opened a few windows. It was Eustace who got the logs there, took up a load on the back of the tractor . . . left the milk and the eggs at the same time. We thought you wouldn't have had time to do much before you went to London . . . dismal it is coming home to a dirty house; couldn't let you do that."

"We'd have come before, but we thought it was Mrs. Lingard . . ."

"Want to see Eustace, do you? He's up in the vegetable garden at the back, digging me a bucket of potatoes." She smiled down at Cara. "Do you like the little pussy cat?"

"Yes, she's sweet."

"She's got kittens in the barn. Do you want to go and see them?"

"Will she mind?"

"She won't mind. Come along, Mrs. Thomas will show you where to find them."

She made for the barn, with the children at her heels; not a backward glance did they spare for their mother, so intent were they on seeing the kittens. Left alone, Virginia went up on the garden path, through a wicket gate, arched in ivy. Eustace's blue shirt could be glimpsed beyond the pea-vines, and she made her way towards this and found him forking up a drill of potatoes. Round and white and smooth as sea pebbles, they were, caked in earth the same colour and consistency as rich, dark chocolate cake.

"Eustace."

He looked over his shoulder and saw her. She waited for him to smile, but he did not. She wondered if he had taken offence. He straightened up, leaning on the handle of the spade.

"Hallo," he said, as though it were a surprise to see her there.

"I've come to say thank you. And I'm sorry."

He shifted the spade from one hand to another. "What have you got to be sorry for?"

"I didn't realize it was you who'd brought the wood and lit the fire and everything. I thought it was Alice Lingard. That's why we haven't been down before."

"Oh, that," said Eustace and she wondered if there was something else she should be sorry about.

"It was terribly kind. The milk and the eggs and everything. It just made all the difference." She stopped, terrified of sounding insincere. "But how did you get into the house?"

Eustace drove the prongs of the fork into the ground, and started towards her. "There's a key here. When my mother was first married, she used to go over sometimes, do a bit of work for old Mr. Crane. His wife was ailing, my mother used to clean the place up. He gave her a key to hang on the dresser and it's been there ever since."

He reached her side, and stood, looking down at her, then he suddenly smiled, his blue eyes crinkled with amusement and she knew that her fears were unjustified, and that he bore no grudge. He said, "So you decided to take the house after all."

Ruefully, Virginia said, "Yes."

"I felt badly, saying those things, and you so upset about everything. I lost my temper, but I shouldn't have."

"You were right. It was all I needed to make me make up my own mind."

"That's why I brought up the logs and stuff . . . I thought it was the least I could do. You'll be wanting more milk . . ."

"Could you let us have it every day?"

"If someone comes and fetches it."

"I could, or one of the children. I hadn't realized, but over the fields and the stiles it's no distance at all."

They had begun to walk back towards the gate.

"Are your children here?"

"They've gone with Mrs. Thomas to see some kittens."

Eustace laughed. "They'll fall in love with them, so be warned. That little tabby got caught by a Siamese up the road, and you've never seen such pretty kittens." He opened the gate for Virginia to go through. "Blue eyes they've got and . . ."

He stopped, watching over her head as Cara and Nicholas came, slowly, carefully, out of the barn, their cupped hands held cradled to their chests, their heads bent in adoration. "What did I tell you?" said Eustace and shut the gate behind them.

The children came up the slope of the lawn, ankle deep, knee deep, in plantains and great white daisies. And all at once Virginia saw them with fresh eyes, with Eustace's eyes, as though she were seeing them for the first time. The fair head and the dark, the blue eyes and the brown. And the sun blinked on to Cara's spectacles so that they flashed like the headlights of a little car, and their new jeans, bought too big, slipped down over their hips and Nicholas's shirt-tail hung out over his firm, round little bottom.

A love-like pain caught at Virginia's throat, unshed tears prickled at the back of her eyes. They were so defenceless, so vulnerable, and for some reason it mattered so much that they should make a good impression on Eustace.

Nicholas caught sight of her. "Look what we've got, Mummy; Mrs. Thomas said that we could bring them out."

"Yes," said Cara, "and they're tiny and they've got their eyes . . ." She saw Eustace, behind her mother, and stopped dead, where she was standing, her face closed up, her eyes watching him from behind her glasses.

But Nicholas came on . . . "Look, Mummy you've got to look. It's all furry and it's got tiny claws. But I don't know if it's a boy or girl. Mrs. Thomas says she can't tell." He looked up and saw Eustace and smiled engagingly into his face. "They've stopped sucking their mother, Mrs. Thomas says, she was getting too thin, and she's put a little saucer of milk out for them, and they lap and their tongues are tiny," he told Eustace.

Eustace put out a long brown finger and scratched the top of the kitten's head. Virginia said, "Nicholas, this is Mr. Philips, you're meant to say how do you do."

"How do you do. Mrs. Thomas said that if we wanted one we could have one but we had to ask you, but you wouldn't mind, would you, Mummy? It's so little and it could sleep on my bed and I'd look after it."

Virginia found herself coming out with all the classic arguments produced by the parents of children, in the same situation as herself. *Too young to be taken from its mother yet. Still needs her to keep him warm. Only at Bosithick for the holidays, and think how he'd hate the train journey back to Scotland.*

Eustace had put down the bucket of potatoes and now went over to where Cara stood, clutching her kitten. Virginia, in agony for her, saw Eustace squat to Cara's height, loosen her fingers gently with his own. "You don't want to hold him too tight, otherwise he won't be able to breathe."

"I'm frightened of dropping him."

"You won't drop him. He wants to look out and see what's happening in the world. He's never seen sun as bright as that." He smiled at the kitten, at Cara. After a little, slowly, she smiled back, and you forgot the ugly spectacles and the bumpy forehead and the straight hair, and saw only the marvellous sweetness of her expression.

After a little he sent them to put the kittens back, and, telling

Virginia to stay outside in the sunshine, went into the house with the potatoes for Mrs. Thomas, only to emerge a moment or so later with a packet of cigarettes and a bar of chocolate. They lay where they had lain before, in the long grass, and were joined there by the children.

He gave them the chocolate but talked to them like adults. What have you been doing? What did you do yesterday in all that rain? Have you been swimming yet?

They told him, voices chiming against each other, Cara, her shyness over, as eager to impart information as Nicholas.

"We bought raincoats, and we got *drenched*. And Mummy had to go to the bank to get more money, and Nicholas got a bucket and spade."

"But I haven't been to the beach to dig yet!"

"And we swam this morning at Mrs. Lingard's. We swam in her pool. But we haven't swum in the sea yet."

Eustace raised his eyebrows. "You haven't swum in the sea and you haven't been to a beach? That's all wrong!"

"Mummy says there hasn't been time . . ."

"But she promised me," Nicholas reminded of his grievance, became indignant. "She said today I could dig with the spade, but I've not been near one grain of sand."

Virginia began to laugh at him, and he became, naturally, angrier than ever. "Well, it's true, and it's what I want more than anything."

"Well," said Eustace, "if you want it more than anything, what are we doing sitting around here talking our heads off?"

Nicholas stared at Eustace, his eyes narrowed suspiciously. "You mean go to the beach?"

"Why not?"

"Now?" Nicholas could not believe his ears.

"Is there anything else you'd rather do?"

"No. Nothing. Nothing else." He sprang to his feet. "Where shall we go? Shall we go to Porthkerris?"

"No, we don't want to go there—nasty crowded place. We'll go to our own private beach, the one that nobody knows about, that belongs to Penfolda and Bosithick."

Virginia was astonished. "I didn't know we had one. I thought there was nothing but cliffs."

By now Eustace was also on his feet. "I'll show you . . . come along, we'll take the Land-Rover."

"My bucket and spade's at our house."

"We'll pick them up on the way."

"And our swimming things," said Cara.

"Those too."

He went into the house to fetch his own things, shouted a message to Mrs. Thomas, led the way through the gate and back across the farmyard. He whistled and the dogs, barking, came rushing around the side of the barn, knowing that the whistle meant a walk, smells, rabbits, maybe a swim. Everybody, including the dogs, clambered into the Land-Rover, and Cara, her shyness now quite forgotten, screamed with delight, as they lurched out of the cobbled farmyard, and went bumping and bouncing up the lane towards the main road.

"Is it far?" she asked Eustace.

"No distance at all."

"What's the beach called?"

"Jack Carley's cove. And it's not a place for babies, only for big children who can look after themselves and climb down the cliff."

They assured him hastily that they came into this category and Virginia watched Nicholas's face, and saw the joyful satisfaction upon it at being indulged, at last, in the one thing he had been wanting to do for a whole day. And what was more, doing it instantly. Not told maybe, or tomorrow, or to wait or to be patient. And she knew exactly how he felt for long ago Eustace had done the very same, performed the same miracle for the young Virginia; had bought her the ice-cream she had been yearning for, and then, out of the blue, asked her to come back to Penfolda.

Chapter 7

THEY LEFT the Land-Rover in the deserted farmyard below Bosithick and started to walk down towards the sea. At first, crossing the fields, they went in a bunch, four abreast, Eustace taking Nicholas by the hand because he was inclined to lag. But then the fields gave way to brambles and bracken and they fell into single file with Eustace leading the way; over crumbling stone walls and across a stream, where rushes grew shoulder high to a small person. Then over another wall, and the path disappeared beneath a jungle of green bracken. Through this they pushed their way, gorse bushes pressing in at either side. The ground all at once slid steeply away from beneath their feet, and the path zig-zagged down through the undergrowth, down to the very lip of the curving cliff. And beyond, space. Blue air. Soaring, screaming gulls, and the distant creaming of the sea.

At this point the coast seemed to fling itself out into a jagged headland, composed of great granite outcrops. Between these the turf was smooth and very green, stained with patches of purple-belled heather, and the path wound down between these outcrops and as they followed its convolutions, a little cove, sheltered and enclosed, gradually revealed itself, far below. The sea was deep and still, purple over the rocks and jade green over the sand. The beach was tiny, and backed by the remains of an old sea wall. Beyond this the land sloped up to the green wedge of the cliff, down which trickled, in a series of small waterfalls, a fresh-water stream. And above the sea wall, tucked snug against the foot of the cliff, stood the remains of a cottage; derelict, windows broken, slates torn from the roof.

They stood in a row, the four of them, buffeted by the gentle wind, looking down. It was a disturbing sensation. Virginia wondered if the children might suffer from vertigo, but neither of them seemed in the least disturbed by the dizzy emptiness of the great height.

"There's a house," said Cara.

"That was where Jack Carley lived."

"Where does he live now?"

"With the angels, I reckon."

"Did you know him?"

"Yes, I knew him. He was an old man when I was a boy. Didn't like people coming down here. Not any old people. Had a great barking dog and he used to chase them away."

"But he let you come?"

"Oh, yes, he let me come." He grinned down at Nicholas. "Do you want me to carry you, or can you manage?"

Nicholas peered out and over. The path trickled down the face of the cliff and so out of sight. Nicholas remained undismayed.

"No. I don't want to be carried, thank you. But I'd like it better if you went first."

In fact, the dogs went first, unafraid, sure-footed as goats. The humans followed at a more prudent speed, but Virginia found that the path was not as dangerous as it appeared. After the dry spell the ground was hard and firm underfoot, and in steep places, steps had been cut, shored up with driftwood or fashioned roughly out of cement.

Much sooner than she had expected they were all safely down. Above them, the cliff loomed, dark and cold in the shadow, but when they jumped down on to the beach they came out of the shade and into the sunshine, and the sand was warm, and there was the smell of tar from the little house, and no sound but the gulls and the creaming sea, and the splash of the stream.

There was an air of unreality about the little cove, as though they had somehow strayed out of time and space. The air was still, the sun burning hot, the sand white and the green water clear as glass. The children stripped off their clothes, and took Nicholas's new bucket and spade and went at once to the water's edge, where they began to dig a sand castle, moated and turreted with bucket-shaped towers.

"If the tide comes in it'll wash the whole castle away," said Cara.

"No, it won't, because we're going to make a great huge moat and then the water will go into that."

"If the tide comes in higher than the castle, it's going to wash it away. Like King Canute."

Nicholas considered this. "Well, it won't for ages."

It was the sort of day that they would remember for the rest of their lives. Virginia imagined them, middle-aged, reminiscing, nostalgic.

There was a little cove and a ruined cottage and not another soul but us. And there were two dogs and we had to climb down a suicidal path.

Who took us?

Eustace Philips.

But who was he?

I can't remember . . . he must have been a farmer, some sort of a neighbour.

And they would argue over details.

There was a stream.

No, it was a waterfall.

There was a stream running down the middle of the beach. I can remember it quite clearly. And we dammed it with a sandbank.

But there was a waterfall too. And I had a new spade.

When the tide was high, they all swam, and the water was clear and salt and green and very cold. Virginia had forgotten her cap and her dark hair lay sleek to her head, and her shadow moved across the pebbled sea-bed like some strange new variety of fish. Holding Cara, she floated, drifting between the sea and the sky, with her eyes dazzled by water and sunshine; and the air was cleft with screaming gulls, and always the gentle murmur of breaking waves.

She became very cold. The children showed no signs of chill, however, so she left them with Eustace, and came out of the water, and went to sit on the dry sand, above the high water mark.

She sat on the sand because they had brought no rug, no super-sized bath-towels. And no comb or lipstick, or biscuits or knitting, and no Thermos of tea, and no extra cardigan. And no plum cake or chocolate biscuits, and no money for the donkey rides or the man with the ice-cream.

She was joined at last by Cara, teeth chattering. Virginia wrapped her in a towel and began gently to dry her. "You'll soon be swimming at this rate."

Cara said, "What time is it?"

Her mother squinted up at the sun. "I suppose, nearly five . . . I don't know."

"We haven't had tea yet."

"No, nor we have. And I don't suppose we will either."

"Not have any *tea*?"

"It doesn't matter for once. We'll have supper later on."

Cara made a face, but raised no objections. Nicholas, however, was vociferous in his complaints when he realized that Virginia had brought nothing for him to eat.

"But I'm hungry."

"I'm sorry."

"Nanny always had shivery bites and you haven't got anything."

"I know. I forgot. We were in such a hurry and I never thought of biscuits."

"Well, what am I going to eat?"

Eustace caught the tail end of this conversation as he came, dripping, up the beach. "What's this?" He stopped to pick up a towel.

"I'm very hungry and Mummy hasn't brought anything to eat."

"Too bad," said Eustace unsympathetically.

Nicholas sent him a long, measured look, and turned away, headed in a sulky silence back to his digging, but Eustace caught him by an arm and pulled him gently back and held him against his knees, rubbing at him absently with the towel, rather as though he were fondling one of the dogs.

Virginia said, placatingly, "Anyway, we'll have to go soon, I expect."

"Why?" asked Eustace.

"I thought you had all those cows to milk."

"Bert's doing them."

"Bert?"

"He was at Penfolda today, cleaning out the loose boxes."

"Oh, yes."

"He used to work for my father, he's retired now, but he comes along every alternate Sunday, gives me a hand. He likes to do it, and Mrs. Thomas feeds him a good dinner, and it means I have a few hours to myself."

Nicholas became irritated by the pointless small-talk. He reared around in Eustace's hands, turned up a furious face towards him. "I am *hungry*."

"So am I," said Cara, wistful if not so vehement.

"Well, listen," said Eustace.

They listened. And heard, over the sound of the sea and the gulls, another sound. The soft drumming of an engine, putt-putt-putt, all the time coming closer.

"What is it?"

"You watch and see."

The sound grew louder. Presently around the point they saw approaching a small open boat, white with a blue stripe, riding the waves with a scud of white spray. A stocky figure stood at its stern. Putt-putt, it swung round into the shelter of the cove, and the engine idled down to a steady throb . . .

They all stared. "There you are!" said Eustace, smug as a conjuror who has brought off a difficult trick.

"Who is it?"asked Virginia.

"That's Tommy Bassett from Porthkerris. Come to pick up his lobster pots."

"But he won't have any biscuits," said Nicholas, who would never be diverted from the matter in hand.

"No. But he might have something else. Shall I go and see?"

"All right." But they sounded doubtful.

He put Nicholas aside and went back down the sand and into the sea, diving through the eye of a peacock-coloured wave, and swimming, with a strong and steady crawl, far out to where the boat bobbed. The lobster pots were already being hauled aboard. The fishermen emptied one and dropped it back, and then saw Eustace coming, and stood, watching.

"Hallo there, boy!" His voice carried across the water.

They saw Eustace catch the gunwales with his hands, hang there for a moment, and then with a heave pull himself clean out of the water and into the rocking boat.

"What a long way to swim," said Cara.

Nicholas said, "I hope he isn't going to bring back a lobster."

"Why not?"

"Lobsters have got claws."

In the boat, some discussion seemed to be taking place. But at last Eustace stood up, and they saw that he was carrying some sort of bundle. He let himself overboard and started back, swimming more slowly this time, hampered as he was by his mysterious burden. This proved to be, of all things, a string shopping-bag, but it contained, wet and dripping, a dozen gleaming mackerel.

Nicholas opened his mouth to say, "I don't like fish," but caught Eustace's eye, and closed his mouth and said nothing instead.

"I thought he might have a few," Eustace told them. "He usually puts a line out when he's coming out to the pots." He smiled down at Cara. "Ever eaten mackerel, have you?"

"I don't think so. But," said Cara, "fancy giving you the string bag." To her, this seemed far more amazing than the gift of the mackerel. "Doesn't he want it back again?"

"He didn't say he did."

"Shall we have to take them back to Bosithick."

"What would we do that for? . . . No, we cook them here . . . come on, you can come and help."

And he collected six or seven big stones, round and smooth, and built them into a ring, and he took matches, and a scrap of an old cigarette packet, and some chips of driftwood and straw, and he kindled a fire and sent the children off to find more wood and soon they had a regular bonfire going. And when the wood ash was deep and grey and burned red when you blew on it, he laid the fish there, in a row, and there was a sizzling and a spitting and presently a most delicious smell.

"But we haven't got knives and forks," said Cara.

"Fingers were made before forks."

"But it'll be hot."

She and Nicholas squatted by the fireside, hair on end, naked except for their bathing pants and a coating of sand. They looked like savages, and perfectly content.

Cara watched Eustace's clever hands. "Have you done this before?"

"What, whittled a stick?"

"No, had a fire, and cooked fish."

"Many times. This is the only way to cook mackerel, and eat it, fresh out of the sea."

"Did you use to do this when you were a boy?"

"Yes."

"Was the old man alive then? Jack Carley."

"Yes. He used to come out and sit on the beach and join in the party. Bring a bottle of rum with him and a smelly old pipe and sit there and tell us yarns so hair-raising we could never be quite sure if they were true."

"What sort of yarns?"

"Oh, adventures . . . he'd been all over the world, done everything. Been a cook in a tanker, a lumberjack, built roads and railways, worked in the mines. He was a tin miner, see. A tinner. Went off to Chile, worked there for five years or more, came home a rich man, but all his money was gone within the twelve months, and he was off again."

"But he came back."

"Yes, he came back. Back to Jack Carley's cove." Cara shivered. "You cold?"

"Nanny calls it a ghost going over your grave."

"Put on a sweater then, and that'll keep the ghosts away, and then it'll be time to eat our tea."

And seeing him with her children, Virginia thought of Anthony who had missed so much because he had never wanted to have anything to do with them. If Cara had been pretty, perhaps he would have paid attention to her . . . Cara who longed for attention and love and thought her father the most wonderful being in the world. But she was plain and shy and wore spectacles, and he never endeavoured to hide the fact that he was ashamed of her. And Nicholas . . . with Nicholas it might have been different. When he was old enough, Anthony would have taught him to shoot and play golf and fish, they would have become friends and gone about together. But now Anthony was dead, and none of this would happen and she felt sorry because they would never now remember swimming with him, they would never crouch with him round a camp fire, listening to his stories and watching his clever hands whittle wooden skewers to be used instead of forks.

The sun slipped down out of the sky, shone directly in upon them, and the sea was turned to a liquid dazzle. It would soon be evening and then it would be dark. And Jack Carley had lived here, just as Aubrey Crane had lived at Bosithick. You didn't see them. You didn't hear them. But you knew that they were still around.

It was disturbing, this awareness of the past, but somehow elemental, and so not really frightening. And it was not possible to live in this part of the world as a nervous or a timid person, for, beneath the beauty it was a savage land, and danger lurked everywhere. In the sea, deep and treacherous, with its undertows and unsuspected currents. In the cliffs and caves, so swiftly cut off and submerged by racing tides. Even the quiet fields down which they had walked this afternoon concealed unthought-of horrors; abandoned mine workings, deep pits and shafts, black as wells, lay hidden beneath the bracken. And scraps of fur and feather, and little bleached bones bore witness to the foxes who built their lairs in earthly hollows under the gorse.

And after nightfall the owl set up his predatory hooting, and the badger emerged to tunnel and scavenge. Not for him the thrill of the hunt. He was just as content to push the lid off a dustbin in the middle of the night, causing such a clatter as to waken the farmer's wife in a cold sweat of fright.

"Mummy. It's cooked." Cara's voice broke across her thoughts. She looked up and saw Cara holding a stick aloft, a fragment of fish impaled dangerously upon its point. "Come and get it *quickly* before it falls off!" Her voice was agonized, and Virginia got to her feet, dusting the sand off the seat of her bathing-suit, and went down to join in the picnic.

In the afterglow of the setting sun, with the offshore wind cool on their faces, they climbed slowly home. After the swim the children were sleepy and silent. Nicholas was not too proud to accept a piggy-back from Eustace, and Virginia carried the wet bathing things and towels in the string bag which had been used for the mackerel, and helped Cara along with the other hand. They were all sandy, salty, tousled, weary, and the path was steep and the climb, up through the bracken and the treacherous undergrowth, exhausting. But at last they reached the fields at the top, and after that the going was easy. Behind them the sea, luminous, in the half-light, reflected all the colours of the sky, and ahead was Bosithick, cradled in the curve of the hill, with the road behind it flickering, every now and then, with the searchlight glare of a passing car.

Some of Eustace's cows had strayed through a gap in the hedge into the top field. In the dusk they loomed, brown and white, and made pleasant munching sounds, raising their heads to watch as the small procession walked by.

Nicholas said, leaning forward to speak into Eustace's ear, "Are you going to come back with us?"

He smiled. "Time I was getting home."

"We would like you to stay for supper."

"You've had your supper," Eustace told him.

"I thought that was tea."

"Don't tell me you've got room for more food."

Nicholas yawned. "No, maybe not."

Virginia said, "I'll make you cocoa, and you can drink it in bed."

"Yes," said Nicholas. "But it would be nice if Eustace would come and talk to us while we had our baths . . ."

Cara chimed in. "Yes, and then Mummy could get our cocoa ready, and you could talk to us."

"I'll do more than that," said Eustace. "I'll scrub the sand off your backs."

They giggled in a high-pitched fashion as though this were very funny, and as soon as they were indoors raced for the bathroom to fight over the taps. Ominous splashing sounds came from beyond the door, and Eustace, rolling up his sleeves, moved in to break it up. Virginia heard him saying, "Quiet now, you'll sink the ship if you don't watch out."

Leaving him to it, she carried the fishy string bag out to the kitchen and emptied the bathing things and the sand-encrusted towels into the sink, and rinsed them out and wrung them, and carried them out into the dark garden, and, by feel, found the clothes-line and pegged them out, leaving them to billow and flap like ghosts in the darkness.

Back in the kitchen, she poured milk into a sauce-pan, put it on to heat, stood watching it, leaning against the cooker, yawning a little. She put up a hand to her eyes, and found that her face was rough with sand, so she took the little mirror out of her handbag, and a comb, and propped the mirror on one of the shelves of the dresser and tried to do something about her hair, but it was stiff and dry with salt, and full of sand. She thought that if there had been a shower, she would have washed it, but the idea of putting it under a tap was somehow all too difficult, too complicated. In the inadequate light her reflection gazed back at her from the round mirror, and there were freckles across the bridge of her nose, but her eyes were shadowed, dark as two holes in her face.

The milk rose in the pan. She made the two mugs of cocoa, put them on a tray, started upstairs with them. She saw that the bathroom was empty, a trail of damp towels and footprints led upstairs. She heard voices and came along the passage, and their bedroom door stood open.

They were inside and they did not see her. She stood and watched them. Eustace sat, with his back to her, on Cara's bed, and the children were perched on Nicholas's bed. All three heads together, Eustace was being given a guided tour of Cara's photographs.

"And this is Daddy. The big one here. He's terribly good-looking, don't you think? . . ." This was Cara, as chatty now as she could be with someone with whom she was completely at ease. "And this is our house in Scotland, that's my bedroom, and that's Nicholas's bedroom, and that's the nursery up at the top . . ."

"That's my bedroom!"

"I said it was that bedroom, silly. And this is Nanny's room, and that's Mummy's room, but you can't see the rooms at the back because they're round at the back. And this is an aerial view . . ."

"A man took it in an aeroplane . . ."

"And that's all the park and the river. And that's the walled garden."

"And that's Mr. McGregor on his tractor, and that's Bob and that's Fergie."

Eustace was beginning to lose the thread . . . "Hold on now, who are Bob and Fergie?"

"Well, Bob helps Mr. McGregor and Fergie helps the gardener. Fergie plays the bagpipes and do you know who taught him? His uncle. And do you know what his uncle is called? Muncle." Nicholas triumphantly produced the answer.

Eustace said, "Uncle Muncle."

"And this is Daddy skiing at St. Moritz, and that's all of us at a grouse shoot—at least, we went to the picnic bit, we didn't go up the hill. And that's the bit of the river where we sometimes swim, but it's not always very safe, and the stones hurt your feet. But Mummy says we can have a swimming pool, she says when we go back to Kirkton, we can have a swimming pool, just like Aunt Alice Lingard's . . ."

"And that's Daddy's car, it's a great big Jaguar. It's a . . ." Nicholas faltered. "It was a great big Jaguar." He finished bravely, "Green."

Virginia said, "Here's your cocoa."

"Oh Mummy, we were showing Eustace all the photographs of Kirkton . . ."

"Yes, I heard."

"That was very nice," said Eustace. "Now I know all about Scotland."

He stood up, as though to get out of Virginia's way, and went to put the photograph frame back on to the chest of drawers.

The children climbed into bed. "You'll have to come and see us. You'll have to come and stay. Won't he, Mummy? He can sleep in the spare room, can't he?"

"Maybe," said Virginia. "But Eustace is a busy man."

"That's it," said Eustace. "Busy. Always got plenty to do. Well . . ." He moved towards the open door. "I'll say good night."

"Oh, good night, Eustace. And thank you for taking us to that lovely place."

"Don't dream about Jack Carley."

"Even if I do I shan't be frightened."

"That's the way. Good night, Nicholas."

"Good night. I'll see you in the morning."

Virginia said to him, "Don't go. I'll be down in a moment."

He said, "I'll wait downstairs."

The cocoa was duly consumed, between yawns. Their eyes drooped. At last they lay down and Virginia kissed them good night. But when she kissed Nicholas he did a surprising thing. Most undemonstrative of children, he put his arms around her neck and held her cheek down against his own.

She said, gently, "What is it?"

"It was a nice place, wasn't it?"

"You mean the little beach?"

"No. The house where Eustace lives."

"Penfolda."

"Will we go back?"

"Sure to."

"I loved that little kitten."

"I know you did."

"Eustace is downstairs."

"Yes."

"I shall hear you talking." His voice was filled with satisfaction. "I shall hear you go talk, talk, talk."

"Will that be cosy?"

"I think so," said Nicholas.

They were near to sleep, but still she stayed with them, moving quickly about the room, picking up stray clothes and folding them and putting them, neat as Nanny, across the seats of the two rickety cane chairs. This done, she went to close the window a little, for the night air was growing chill, to draw the skimpy curtains. The room, by the meagre light of the bedside lamp was all at once enclosed, safe, soft with shadows, the only sound the ticking of Cara's clock and the breathing of the children.

She was filled, in that moment, with love. For her children; for this strange little house; for the man, downstairs, who waited for her. And aware, too, of a marvellous sense of completion, of rightness. It will be the first time, she thought, that Eustace and I have been alone, with all the time in the world. Just the two of us. She would light the fire for company and draw the curtains and make him a jug of coffee. If they wished, they could talk all night. They could be together.

Cara and Nicholas were sleeping. She turned off the light and went downstairs to unexpected and surprising darkness. For an incredulous moment she thought that Eustace had changed his mind and already gone, but then she saw that he stood by the window, smoking, watching the very last of the light fade from the sky. A little of this light was reflected upon his face, but when he heard her footstep he turned, and she could see no expression on his face, only shadows.

She said, "I thought you'd gone."

"No. I'm still here."

The darkness disturbed her. She reached for the lamp on the table and switched it on. Yellow light was thrown, like a pool, between them. She waited for him to speak, but when he said nothing, simply stood there, smoking, she began to fill the silence with words.

"I . . . I don't know about supper. Do you want something to eat? I don't even know what time it is."

"I'm all right."

"I could make you some coffee . . ."

"You haven't got a can of beer?"

She made a helpless gesture. "I haven't, Eustace. I'm sorry. I never bought any. I never drink it." That sounded priggish, as though she disapproved of beer. "I mean, I just don't like the taste." She smiled, trying to turn it into a joke.

"It doesn't matter."

The smile collapsed. Virginia swallowed. "Are you sure you wouldn't like coffee?"

"No, thank you." He began to look about for somewhere to stub out his cigarette. She found him a saucer and put it on the table, and he demolished the stub as through he had a personal, vicious grudge against it.

"I must go."

"But . . ."

He turned towards her, waiting for her to finish. She lost her nerve. "Yes. It's been a good day. It was kind of you to give up your day for us and show us the cove and . . . everything." Her voice sounded high-pitched and formal as though she were opening a sale of work. "The children loved it."

"They're good children."

"Yes. I . . ."

"When are you going back to Scotland?"

The abruptness of the question, the coldness of his voice, were shocking. She was suddenly cold, a shiver of apprehension trickling down her spine like a stream of icy water.

"I . . . I'm not sure." She took hold of the back of one of the wooden chairs, leaning against it as if for support. "Why do you ask?"

"You're going to go back."

It was a statement, not a question. Faced with it, Virginia's natural diffidence leapt to the worst conclusion. Eustace expected her to go, even wanted her to go. She heard herself telling him, with marvellous lightness, "Well, some time, of course. After all, it's my home. The children's home."

"I hadn't realized until this evening that it was such a considerable property . . ."

"Oh, you mean, Cara's photographs . . ."

"But then, you have plenty of people to help you run it."

"I don't run it, Eustace."

"Then you should. Learn something about farming. You'd be surprised how much there is to it. You should take an interest, start up something new. An Aberdeen Angus herd. Did your husband ever think of doing that? You can sell a good bull at the Perth sales for sixty, seventy thousand pounds?"

It was like a conversation in a nightmare, mad and pointless. She said, "Can you?" but her mouth was dry and the words scarcely made any sound at all.

"Of course. And who knows, one day you may have built up something really great to hand on to that boy of yours."

"Yes."

He said again, "I must go." The trace of a smile crossed his features. "It was a good day."

But Virginia remembered a better one, that other day she had spent with Eustace, the spring afternoon of sun and wind when he had brought her an ice-cream and finally driven her home. And he had promised to telephone her, and then forgotten, or perhaps he had changed his mind. She realized that she had been waiting, all afternoon, for him to tell her what really happened. She had been expecting him to bring up the subject, perhaps as a story for the children to share, or as a scrap of harmless nostalgia to be remembered, over the years, by two old friends. But he had said nothing. And now she would never know.

"Yes." She let go of the chair and straightened up, folding her arms across her chest as though she were trying to stay warm. "A special day. The kind that people never forget."

He moved towards her, around the edge of the table, and Virginia turned away from him and went to open the door. Cool air, smelling sweet and damp, flooded in from a night arched in a sapphire sky, bright with stars. Out of the darkness a curlew sent up its long mournful cry.

He was beside her. "Good night, Virginia."

"Good night, Eustace."

And then he was going down the steps, away from her, over the wall and down the fields towards the old farmyard where he had left his car. The dusk swallowed him. She closed the door and locked it and went back to the kitchen and took the children's cocoa mugs and washed them, slowly and carefully. She heard his Land-Rover go grinding up past the gate, up the lane towards the main road, heard the sound of the engine die away into the quiet night, but she never looked up from what she was doing. When the mugs were dry, the tea towel folded and there was nothing more to do, she found that she was exhausted. She turned off the lights and went slowly upstairs and undressed and climbed into bed. Her body lay slack, but the inside of her head behaved as though she had been living on black coffee for a week.

He doesn't love you.

I never thought he did.

But you were beginning to think so. After today.

Then I was wrong. We have no future together. He made that very clear.

What did you imagine was going to happen?

I imagined that he would be able to talk about what happened ten years ago.

Nothing happened. And why should he remember?

Because I did. Because Eustace was the most important person, the most important thing that ever happened to me.

You didn't remember. You married Anthony Keile.

They were married in London, in July; Virginia in a cream satin dress with a six foot train and a veil that had belonged to Lady Keile's grandmother, and Anthony in a grey frock-coat and an immaculately cut pair of sponge-bag trousers. They emerged from St. Michael's, Chester Square, with bells jangling, sun shining, and a small retinue of beribboned bridesmaids extorting *oohs* and *aahs* of admiration from the thin crowd of inquisitive women who had realized that there was a wedding going on, and hung about to see what turned up when the doors were opened.

The excitement, the champagne, the pleasures of being loved and congratulated and kissed kept Virginia going until it was time to go upstairs and change. Her mother was there, ubiquitous, efficient, to unzip the clinging satin and unpin the borrowed tiara and the filmy veil.

"Oh, my dear, it all went off so beautifully, and you really did look enchanting, even though perhaps I shouldn't say anything so conceited about my own child . . . Darling, you're shivering, you're surely not cold?"

"No. I'm not cold."

"Change your shoes, then, and I'll help you on with your dress."

It was rose pink, with a tiny petalled hat to match, a charming useless ensemble that she would never wear again. She imagined coming back from her honeymoon, still wearing paper silk and pink petals, a little crushed by now, and going brown at the edges. (But of course they couldn't go brown, they weren't real, they were pretence petals . . .)

"And your suitcase is in the boot of Anthony's car, such a good idea taking a taxi round to the flat and picking the car up there, then you have none of this terrible horse-play with kippers and old shoes."

A roar, a galloping of feet, came from the passage outside the bedroom. Anthony's voice was raised in a comic sound like a hunting horn. "There! He sounds as though he's ready." She kissed Virginia briskly. "Have a good time, my darling."

The door burst open, and Anthony stood there, wearing the suit that he had chosen to go away in, and with a large sun hat on the top of his head. He was considerably drunk.

"Here she is! We're off to the South of France, my love, which is why I am wearing this hat."

Mrs. Parsons, laughing indulgently, removed it, smoothed his hair with her long fingers, straightened his tie. She might have been the bride, not Virginia, who stood and watched this little ceremony with a face that held no expression whatsoever. Anthony held out a hand to her. "Come on," he said. "Time we went."

The hired car, awash in confetti, took them back to the Parsons' flat, where Anthony's car was waiting for them. The plan had been that they should get straight into his car and drive to the airport, but Virginia had a latch-key in her purse, and instead, they let themselves in and went into the kitchen, and she tied an apron around the pink silk dress, and Anthony sat on the table and watched while she brewed him up a jug of black coffee.

For their honeymoon they had been lent a villa in Antibes. By their second day Anthony had met an old friend; by the end of the first week, he knew everyone in the place. Virginia told herself that this was what she had expected, was what she wanted. Anthony's gregarious instincts were part of his charm, and one of the things that had attracted her to him in the first place. Besides, after one day it became very obvious that they were going to find it hard to think of things to say to each other. Conversation at meals was inclined to be distinctly sticky. She realized then, that they had never been alone together before now.

There was a couple, called Janey and Hugh Rouse; he was a writer and they had rented a house at Cap Ferrat. Janey was older than Virginia and Virginia liked her, and found her easy to talk to. Once, sitting on the terrace at the Rouses's house, waiting for the men to come up from the rocks, Janey had said, "How long have you known Anthony, honey?" She had lived, as a child, in the States, and although she did not speak with an American accent, her speech was spattered with words and phrases which instantly gave her origins away.

"Not very long. I met him in May."

"Love at first sight, hm?"

"I don't know. I suppose so."

"How old are you?"

"Eighteen."

"That's awfully young to settle down. Not that I can see that Anthony settling down too much for a few years yet."

"He'll have to," Virginia told her. "You see, we're going to live in Scotland. Anthony's been left this estate, Kirkton . . . it used to belong to an uncle who was a bachelor. And we're going to go and live there."

"You mean, you think Anthony will spend all his time tramping around in a tweed suit with mud on his boots?"

"Not exactly. But I can't believe that living in Scotland is going to be quite the same as living in London."

"It won't," said Janey, who had been there. "But don't expect the simple life, or you'll be disappointed."

But Virginia did expect the simple life. She had never seen Kirkton, never been to Scotland for that matter, but she had once spent an Easter holiday with a schoolfriend who lived in Northumberland and somehow she imagined that Scotland would be rather like that, and that Kirkton would be a low-ceilinged, rambling, stone farmhouse, with flagged floors, and worn Turkey carpets, and a diningroom with a great log fire and hunting prints on the walls.

Instead, she was presented with a tall, square, elegantly proportioned Adam house, with sash windows full of reflected sunshine, and a flight of stone stairs which led, from the carriage sweep, up to the front door.

Beyond the gravel was grass, and then a ha-ha wall, and then the park, landscaped with giant beeches, sloping down to the distant silver curve of the river.

Overwhelmed, silent, Virginia had followed Anthony up the steps and through the door. The house was empty, old-fashioned and unfurnished. Between them they were going to do it up. To Virginia the task seemed daunting, but when she said as much Anthony overrode her.

"We'll get Philip Sayer on to it, he's this interior decorator my mother got to do the house in London for her. Otherwise we'll make the most ghastly mistakes and the place will be a mess."

Virginia privately thought she preferred her own glastly mistakes to somebody else's impeccable taste—it was more homely; but she said nothing.

"And this is the drawing-room, and then the library beyond. And the dining-room, and there are kitchens and stuff downstairs."

The room soared and echoed, the icy prisms of crystal chandeliers glinted, dependent from ornately decorated ceilings. There was panelling and marvelous cornices over the tall windows. There was dust and a distinct feeling of chill.

They mounted to the first floor up a curved stairway, airy and elegant, and their steps echoed on the polished treads and through the empty house. Upstairs, there were bedrooms, each with its own bathroom, dressing-rooms, linen rooms, housemaid's cupboards, even a boudoir.

"What would I do with a boudoir?" Virginia wanted to know.

"You can come and boud in it, and if you don't know what that means, it's French for sulk. Oh, come on, take that horrified expression off your face and look as though you're enjoying yourself."

"It's just so big."

"You talk as though it were Buckingham Palace."

"I've never been in such a big house. I certainly never thought I would live in one."

"Well, you're going to, so you'd better get used to it."

Eventually they were outside again, standing by the car, staring up at the elegant front elevation, regularly spaced with windows. Virginia put her hands deep in the pockets of her coat and said, "Where's the garden?"

"What do you mean?"

"I mean flower-beds and stuff. Flowers. You know. A garden."

But the garden was a half-mile away, enclosed in a wall. They drove there and went inside and found a gardener and rows of fruit and vegetables like soldiers, waiting to be picked off.

"This is the garden," said Anthony.

"Oh," said Virginia.

"What's that meant to mean?"

"Nothing. Just oh."

The interior decorator duly arrived. Hard on his heels came vans and lorries, builders, plasterers, painters, men with carpets, men with curtains, men in pan-technicons which spilled out furniture like cornucopias, endlessly, as though they would never run out.

Virginia let it all happen. "Yes," she would say, agreeing to whatever shade of velvet Philip Sayer was suggesting. Or "Yes" when he thought of Victorian brass bedsteads in the spare room, and thick white crochet bedcovers. "Terribly Osborne, my dear, you know, Victorian Country Life."

The only time that she had raised her voice with an independent idea was over the kitchen. She wanted it like the one she remembered, the marvellous room at Penfolda with its air of stability, the suggestion in the air of good things cooking, the cat in the chair and the geraniums crowded on the window-sill.

"A farmhouse kitchen! That's what I want. A farmhouse kitchen's like a living-room."

"Well, I'm not going to live in any kitchen, I'll tell you that."

And she had let Anthony have his way because, after all, it was not her house, and it was not her money which paid for the stainless steel sinks, and the black and white floor and the patent self-cleaning cooking unit with eye-level grill, and a spit for broiling chickens.

It was finished and Virginia was pregnant.

"How marvellous for Nanny!" said Lady Keile.

"Why?"

"Well, darling, she's in London, doing temporary work, but she's longing, but longing for a new baby. Of course she won't be all that keen on leaving London, but she's bound to make friends, you know what this Nanny's network's like, better than the English Speaking Union I always say. And that top floor is *meant* to be a nursery, you can tell by the gate at the top of the stairs, and the bars on the windows. Gorgeously sunny. I think pale blue, don't you? For carpets, I mean, and then French chintz curtains . . ."

Virginia tried to stand up for herself. To say, *No. I will look after my own baby.* But she was so sick carrying Cara, so weak and unwell, that by the time she once again felt strong enough to cope with the situation and stand on her own two feet, the nursery had been decorated and Nanny was there, established, rigid, immovable.

I'll let her stay. Just until the baby's born and I'm on my feet again. She can stay for a month or two, and then I'll tell her that she can go back to London because I want to look after my baby for myself.

But by then, there were further complications. Virginia's mother, in London, complained of pains and tiredness; she thought she was losing weight. Virginia at once went south to see her, and after that, her loyalties were torn between her baby in Scotland and her mother in London. Travelling up and down in the train it became very clear that it would be madness to get rid of Nanny until Mrs. Parsons had recovered. But of course, she didn't recover and, by the time the whole ghastly nightmare was over, Nicholas had arrived and, with two babies in the nursery, Nanny was dug in for good.

At Kirkton they were surrounded, within a radius of ten miles or so, by a number of entertaining neighbours. Young couples with time and money to spare, some with young children like the Keiles', all with interests which matched Anthony's.

For appearances' sake, he put in a certain amount of time on the farm, talking to McGregor, the grieve, finding out what McGregor thought should be done, and then telling McGregor to do it. The rest of the day was his own, and he used it to the full, doing exactly what he wanted. Scotland is a country geared to the pleasures of menfolk, and there was always shooting to be got, grouse in the summer, and partridges and pheasants in the autumn and winter. There were rivers to be fished and golf courses and a social life which was even gayer than the one he had left behind in London.

Virginia did not fish or play golf and Anthony would not have invited her to join him even if she had wanted to. He preferred the company of his men-friends, and she was expected to be present only when they had been invited specifically as a couple. To a dinner or a dance, or perhaps to lunch before a point-to-point, when she would go through agonies trying to decide what to put on, and inevitably turn up in what everybody had been wearing last year.

She was still shy. And she didn't drink so there seemed no artificial way of getting over this terrible defect. The men, Anthony's friends, obviously thought her a bore. And their wives, though kind and friendly, terrified her with their private jokes and their incomprehensible references to places and persons and events known only to them. They were like a lot of girls who had all been to the same school.

Once, driving home after a dinner party, they quarrelled. Virginia had not meant to quarrel but she was tired and unhappy, and Anthony was more than a little drunk. He always seemed to drink too much at parties, almost as though it were a social grace that was expected of him. This evening it made him aggressive and bad-tempered.

"Well, did you enjoy yourself?"

"Not particularly."

"You certainly didn't look as though you did."

"I was tired."

"You're always tired. And yet you never seem to do a thing."

"Perhaps that's why I'm tired."

"And what does that mean?"

"Oh, nothing."

"It has to mean something."

"All right, it means that I get bored and lonely."

"That's not my fault."

"Isn't it? You're never there . . . sometimes you're not in the house all day. You have lunch in the club at Relkirk . . . I never see you."

"OK. Me and about a hundred other chaps. What do you suppose their wives do? Sit and mope?"

"I've wondered what they do with their time. You tell me."

"Well, they get around, that's what. They see each other, take the children to Pony Club meets, play bridge; I suppose, garden."

"I can't play bridge," said Virginia, "and the children don't want to ride ponies, and I would garden only there isn't a garden at Kirkton, just a four-walled prison for flowers, and a bad-tempered gardener who won't let me so much as cut a bunch of gladioli without asking him first."

"Oh, for heaven's sake . . ."

She said, "I watch other people. Ordinary couples, sometimes on Saturdays in Relkirk. Doing the shopping together in the rain or the sunshine, and children with them, sucking ice-creams, and they put all the parcels into shabby little cars and drive home, and they look so happy and cosy, all together."

"Oh, God. You can't want that."

"I want not to be lonely."

"Loneliness is a state of mind. Only you can do anything about that."

"Weren't you ever lonely, Anthony?"

"No."

"Then you didn't marry me for company. And you didn't marry me for my startling conversation."

"No." Coldly agreeing, his profile was stony.

"Then why?"

"You were pretty. You had a certain fawn-like charm. You were very charming. My mother thought you were very charming. She thought your mother was very charming. She thought the whole bloody arrangement was charming."

"But you didn't marry me because your mother told you to."

"No. But you see, I had to marry somebody, and you turned up at such a singularly opportune time."

"I don't understand."

He did not reply to this. For a little he drove in silence, perhaps prompted by some shred of decency not to tell her the truth, now or ever. But Virginia, having come so far, made the mistake of pressing him. "Anthony, I don't understand," and he lost his temper and told her.

"Because I was left Kirkton on condition that I was married when I took it over. Uncle Arthur thought I would never settle down, would break the place up if I moved in as a bachelor . . . I don't know what he thought, but he was determined that if I lived at Kirkton I'd do it as a family man."

"So that's why!"

Anthony frowned. "Are you hurt?"

"I don't think so. Should I be?"

He fumbled for her hand with his own . . . the car swerved slightly as his fingers closed over hers. He said, "It's all right. It may be no better, but it's certainly no worse than other marriages. Sometimes it's a good thing to be frank and clear the air. It's better to know where we both stand."

She said, "Do you ever regret it? Marrying me, I mean."

"No. I don't regret it. I'm just sorry that it had to happen when we were both so young."

One day she found herself in the house alone. Quite alone. It was Saturday, and afternoon. Mr. McGregor, the grieve, had gone to Relkirk, taking Mrs. McGregor with him. Anthony was playing golf, and Nanny and the children were out for a walk. An empty house and nothing to do. No washing to be done, no cake to be baked, no ironing, no garden to weed. Virginia walked through it, going from room to room, as though she were a stranger who had paid to see around, and her footsteps echoed on the polished staircase, and there was the tick of the clock, and everywhere order, neatness. This was what Anthony loved. This was what he had created. This was why he had married her. She ended up in the hall, opened the front door and went down the steps on to the gravel, thinking that she would maybe spy Nanny and the children in the distance; she would go to meet them, run and snatch Cara up in her arms, hug her and hold her, if only to prove that she really existed, that she was not a dream-child that Virginia had conceived, like some frustrated spinster, out of her own imagination.

But there was no sign of Nanny and, after a little, she went back up the steps and so indoors again, because there did not seem to be anywhere else to go.

There was a pretty girl, called Liz, married to a young lawyer who worked in Edinburgh. He worked in Edinburgh, but they lived only a mile or two from Kirkton, in an old, converted Presbyterian manse, with a wild garden, that was filled with daffodils in the spring, and a paddock for the ponies.

She had young children, dogs, a cat, and a parrot in a cage, but—perhaps because she missed her husband who was in Edinburgh all week, or perhaps because she was simply a girl who enjoyed people—her house was always full. Other mothers' children lolloped about on the ponies, crowded the dining-room table at tea-time, played rounders on the lawn. If she didn't have whole families staying with her, then she had whole families for the day, feeding them on huge roasts of beef, and steak and kidney pies, marvellous old-fashioned puddings, and home-made ice-creams. Her drink cupboard, which must have taken a frightening beating from the hordes who passed through her hospitable doorway, was always open, always at hand for any guest in need of a little liquid refreshment.

"Help yourself," she would call through the open door, while she knocked up a three-course dinner for ten unexpected guests. "There's ice in the fridge if the ice-bucket's empty."

Anthony, naturally enough, adored her, flirted cheerfully and openly with her, put on a great show of jealousy when the week-ends came around and her husband was home.

"Get that bloody man out of the house," he would tell Liz, and she would go into gales of delighted laughter, as would everybody else who was listening. Virginia smiled, and over their heads met the eye of Liz's husband. He was a quiet young man, and though he stood there, with a glass in his hand, smiling, it was almost impossible to tell what he was thinking.

"You'll have to watch out for that husband of yours," one of the other wives said to Virginia. But she only said, "I have been, for years," and changed the subject, or turned to speak to somebody else.

One Tuesday, Anthony called her from the club in Relkirk. "Virginia. Look, I've got embroiled in a poker game, God knows when I'll be home. But don't wait, I'll get a bite to eat here. See you later."

"All right. Don't lose too much money."

"I shall win," he told her. "I shall buy you a mink coat."

"That's just what I need."

He arrived home, after midnight, stumbling up the stairs. She heard him moving about in his dressing-room, dropping things, opening and shutting drawers, swearing at some cuff-link or button.

After a little, she heard him getting into bed, and the light beyond the open door went out, and there was only darkness. And she wondered if he had chosen to sleep in his dressing-room out of consideration to Virginia, or whether there was some other, more sinister reason.

She soon knew. The society in which they moved, the narrow clique, was too small for secrets. "Virginia darling, I told you to watch out for that naughty man of yours."

"What's he done now?"

"You are marvellous, the way you never get ruffled. You obviously know all about it."

"All about what?"

"Darling, the intimate dinner party that he had with Liz."

". . . Oh, yes, of course. Last Tuesday."

"He is an old devil. I suppose he thought none of us would find out. But then Midge and Johnny Gray suddenly decided on the spur of the moment to go up to the Strathtorrie Arms for dinner, you know, there's a new manager now, and it's all frightfully dark and chic and you can get a very good dinner. Anyway, off they went, and of course there were Anthony and Liz, all snugged up in a corner. And you knew all the time!"

"Yes."

"Any you don't mind?"

"No."

That was the terrible thing. She didn't mind. She was apathetic, bored by Anthony and the outrageous schoolboy charm that had, as far as Virginia was concerned, long since worn itself to shreds. And this was not the first affair. It had happened before and it would doubtless happen again, but still, it was daunting to look down the years ahead and see herself tied for ever to this tedious Peter Pan. A man so un-perceptive that he could gaily embark on a clandestine involvement, and yet conduct the whole affair on what was virtually his own front doorstep.

She thought about divorce, but knew that she would never divorce Anthony, not simply because of the children, but because she was Virginia, and she could no more embark, voluntarily, upon such a course, than she could have flown to the moon.

She was not happy, but what could be the good of broadcasting her failure, her disillusion, to the rest of the world? Anthony did not love her, had never loved her. But then she had never loved him. If he had married Virginia to get his hands on Kirkton, then she had married Anthony on the rebound, in an emotional state of extreme unhappiness, and in a desperate bid to avoid the London Season that her mother had planned for her, culminating in the final nightmare of a coming-out dance.

She was not happy, but, to all intents and purposes, she had everything. A lovely house, a handsome husband, and the children. The children were worth everything. For them she would shore up her crumbling marriage, and for them she would create a world of security that they would never know again.

Anthony had been with Liz that night he was killed. He had called in at the Old Manse for a drink on his way back from Relkirk and was invited to stay for supper.

He rang Virginia.

"Liz has got the Cannons staying. She wants me to eat here and make up a four for bridge. I'll be home some time. Don't wait up."

Liz's cupboard with the whisky bottle stood open, as always. And as always Anthony helped himself liberally and with a generous hand. It was two o'clock before he started home, a black and starless night of pouring rain. It had been raining for days and the river was in spate. Afterwards the police came with tape measures and bits of chalk, and they measured the skid marks, and hung over the broken rail of the bridge and stared down into the muddy, swirling waters. And Virginia stood with them, in the drenching rain, and watched the divers go down, and there was a kindly sergeant who kept urging her to go back to the house, but she wouldn't go because, for some reason, she had to be there, because he had been her husband and the father of her children.

And she remembered what he had said, that night he told her about Kirkton. *I'm just sorry that it had to happen when we were both so young.*

Chapter 8

THE QUIET NIGHT moved slowly past, the seconds, the minutes, the hours, measured by the ticking of Virginia's wrist-watch which she had put on the table by her bed. Now, she reached out for it and saw that it was nearly three o'clock in the morning. She got out of bed, wrapped herself in the quilt and went to sit on the floor by the open window. It was the hour before dawn, dark and very still. She could hear, a mile or more away, the gentle movement, like breathing, of the sea. She could hear the soft shufflings and munchings of the Guernseys, grazing two or three fields distant; she could hear rustlings and whisperings and creepings from hedgerow and burrow, and the hooting of a night owl.

She found that she was devilled by the memory of Liz. Liz had come to Anthony's funeral wearing a face of grief and guilt so naked that instinctively one had turned away from it, not wanting to witness such pain. Soon afterwards her husband had taken her to the South of France for a holiday and Virginia had not seen her again.

But now she knew that she must go back to Scotland and soon, if it was only to square things up with Liz. To convince Liz that no blame could ever be laid at her door, to make—as far as was humanly possible —friends with her again. She thought of returning to Kirkton and this time her imagination did not turn and run but took the journey quietly and without horror. Off the road it went, and down over the bridge and the river, and up the drive between the lush meadows of the park. It came to the curving sweep in front of the house, and went up the steps and in through the front door, and now there was no longer the old familiar sensation of loneliness, of being trapped. But simply a sadness that the lives of the people who had lived in this beautiful house had achieved no lasting cohesion, but had unravelled like a length of badly spun yarn, and finally shredded away.

She would sell the house. Somewhere, some time, her subconscious had made the decision and now presented it to her conscious mind as a *fait accompli*. How much this phenomenon had to do with Eustace, Virginia could not at the moment comprehend. Later on, no doubt, it would all work itself out. For now the relief was enormous, like the shedding of a load carried too long, and she felt grateful, as though another person had stepped in and made the decision for her.

She would sell Kirkton. Buy another house, a little house . . . somewhere. Again, later on, it would all work itself out. She would make a new home, new friends, create a garden, buy a puppy, a kitten, a canary in a cage. Find schools for the children, fill the holidays with pleasures she had previously been too diffident to attempt. She would learn to ski; they would go on ski-ing holidays together. She would build kites and mend bicycles, let Cara read all the books she ever wanted, and go to Nicholas's sports days wearing the right sort of hat, and achieve marvellous things like winning the egg-and-spoon race.

And it would happen because she would make it happen. There was no more Eustace, no more dreams, but other good things were constant. Like pride, and resolution, and the children. The children. And she smiled, knowing that, like the arrow on the compass for ever pointing north, whatever she did and however she behaved, she was always left, facing squarely in their direction.

She was beginning to be cold. The first lightening of dawn was beginning to creep up into the sky. She got up off the floor, took a sleeping-pill and a glass of water and climbed back into bed. When she opened her eyes again the sun, high in the sky, was shining full in her face, and from downstairs came a terrible racket, a banging at the front door and a voice calling her name.

"Virginia! It's me. Alice! Wake up, or are you all dead?"

Dazed with shock and sleep, Virginia stumbled out of bed, across the floor, and hung out of the window. "Alice! Stop making such a din. The children are asleep."

Alice, foreshortened, turned up an astonished face. Her voice dropped to an exaggerated stage-whisper. "I'd begun to think you'd all passed out. It's past ten. Come down and let me in!"

Yawning, incapable, Virginia groped for her dressing-gown, pushed her feet into slippers and went downstairs, pausing at the open door of the children's room on the way. To her surprise they were still asleep, undisturbed by Alice's shouting. She thought, we must have been late last night. We must have been much later than I realized.

She unlocked the door, to let in a flood of sunshine and Alice. Alice wore a crisp blue linen dress, a silk scarf over her head. As usual she was bright-skinned, clear-eyed, maddeningly awake.

"Do you usually wake up at this hour?"

"No, but . . ." Virginia swallowed a yawn. ". . . I couldn't get to sleep last night. Eventually I took a pill. It must have knocked me out."

"And the children?"

"I didn't give them a pill, but they're still asleep. We were late, we were out all day." She yawned again, forced her eyes open. "How about some coffee?"

Alice looked amused. "You certainly look as though you'll need some. I tell you what. I'll make it, you go and get yourself woken up, and put some clothes on. It's no good talking to you when you're in this state." She laid her handbag on the table in a purposeful way. "I must say, this really isn't too bad a little house, is it? And here's the kitchen. A little poky, perhaps, but perfectly adequate . . ."

Virginia ran a bath, got into it and washed her hair. Afterwards, she went upstairs, wrapped in a towel, and took clean clothes from the drawer, and a cotton dress, as yet unworn, from the wardrobe. She pushed her feet into sandals, combed her sleek wet hair into place, and feeling clean and strangely hungry, went back downstairs to Alice.

She found her thoroughly organized, the kettle on the gas, the jug ready with the coffee, mugs laid out on the table.

"Oh, there you are . . . we're just about ready . . . I thought we'd have proper coffee; I get so fed up with this wishy-washy stuff, don't you?"

Virginia sat on the edge of the table. "When did you get back from London?"

"Last night."

"How was it? Did you have fun?"

"Yes, but I didn't come here to talk about London."

"In that case, what brought you here at ten o'clock on a Monday morning?"

"Curiosity," said Alice. "Sheer, undiluted curiosity."

"About me?"

"About Eustace Philips!"

Virginia said, "I don't understand."

"Mrs. Jilkes told me. I was scarcely in through the front door when I was hearing all about it. She said that Eustace had telephoned her while I was away to ask if anybody was getting Bosithick ready for you and the children. And she said I was in London, and he said not to bother, he'd see to it."

"Yes, that's right . . . and he did too . . ."

"But Virginia . . . You talked about Eustace, but you never told me that you'd met him again."

"Didn't I?" Virginia frowned. "No, I didn't, did I?"

"But when did you meet him?"

"That day I came out to see the cottage. Do you remember? I said I wouldn't be back for lunch. And I went to the pub in Lanyon to buy cigarettes and I met him there."

"But why didn't you say anything about it? Was there any particular reason that you didn't want me to know?"

"No." She tried to remember. "But I suppose I just didn't want to talk about him." She smiled. "It wasn't as though it had been such a friendly reunion. In fact, we had the most terrible row . . ."

"But did you *mean* to meet him again?"

"No. It just happened."

"And he remembered you? After all this time? But he'd only ever seen you that once at the barbecue."

"No," said Virginia. "I did see him again."

"*When?*"

"About a week after the barbecue. I met him in Porthkerris. We spent the afternoon together and he drove me back to Wheal House. You didn't see him because you were out that day. But my mother was there. She knew about it."

"But why was it all kept such a secret?"

"It wasn't a secret, Alice. It was just that my mother didn't like Eustace. I must say, he didn't make much of an effort to impress her, and he was rude and the Land-Rover was covered with bits of straw and mud and manure . . . not my mother's cup of tea at all. She treated the whole incident as though it were a sort of joke, but I knew that he had made her angry, and that she didn't like him."

"But you could have talked to me about him. After all, it was I who introduced you to Eustace."

"I tried, but every time I started, my mother somehow broke into the conversation or changed the subject or interrupted in some way. And . . . you mustn't forget this, Alice . . . you were her friend, not mine. I was just the little girl, out of the nursery. I never imagined for a moment that you'd take my side against hers."

"Was it a question of taking sides?"

"It would have been. You know what a snob she was."

"Oh, yes, of course, but it was harmless."

"No, Alice, it wasn't harmless. It was terribly dangerous. It affected everything she did. It deformed her."

"Virginia!" Alice was shocked.

"That's why we suddenly went back to London. You see, she knew, she guessed right away, that I was in love with Eustace."

The kettle boiled. Alice lifted it, and filled the coffee jug, and the kitchen was suffused with a delicious fresh smell. Alice drew a spoon gently across the surface of the coffee.

"And were you?" she asked at last. "In love with Eustace?"

"Of course I was. Wouldn't you have been at seventeen?"

"But you married Anthony Keile."

"Yes."

"Did you love him?"

"I . . . I married him."

"Were you happy?"

"I was lonely . . ."

"But, Virginia, I always thought . . . I mean, your mother always said . . . I thought you were so happy," Alice finished, hopeless with confusion.

"No. But it wasn't all Anthony's fault. It was my fault, too."

"Did Lady Keile know this?"

"No." Nor did she know the circumstances of Anthony's death. Nor did she know about Liz. Nor was she ever going to. "Why should she know? She used to come and stay with us, but never for more than a week at a time. It wasn't difficult to foster the illusion of an idyllically happy marriage. It was the least we could do for her . . ."

"I'm surprised Nanny never said anything."

"Nanny never saw anything she didn't want to see. And to her, Anthony was perfection."

"It can't have been easy."

"No. but like I said, it wasn't all Anthony's fault."

"And Eustace?"

"Alice, I was seventeen; a little girl, waiting for someone to come and buy her a ice-cream."

"But not now . . ." said Alice.

"No. Now I'm twenty-seven and the mother of two children. And I'm not waiting for ice-creams any longer."

"You mean, he has nothing to give you."

"And he needs nothing from me. He's self-sufficient. He has his own life. He has Penfolda."

"Have you discussed this with him?"

"Oh, Alice . . ."

"You obviously haven't. So how can you be so certain?"

"Because all those years ago, he said he'd phone me. He said that he wanted me to come out to Penfolda for tea or something, to meet his mother again. And I was going to borrow your car and drive myself out here. But you see, he never telephoned. I waited, but he never telephoned. And before there was time to find out why, or do anything about it, I'd been whisked back to London by my mother."

Alice said, "And how do you *know* he never telephoned?" She was beginning to sound impatient.

"Because he never did."

"Perhaps your mother took the call."

"I asked her. And she said there'd never been any telephone call."

"But, Virginia, she was perfectly capable of taking a call and never telling you about it. Specially if she didn't like the young man. Surely you realized that."

Her voice was brisk and practical. Virginia stared, scarcely able to believe her ears. That Alice should say such things about Rowena Parsons—Alice of all people, her mother's oldest friend. Alice, coming out with a dark truth that Virginia had never had the courage to find out for herself. She remembered her mother's face, smiling across the railway carriage, the laughing protest. *"Darling! What an accusation. Of course not. You surely didn't think . . ."*

And Virginia had believed her. She said at last, helplessly, "I thought she was telling me the truth. I didn't think she was capable of lying."

"Let's say she was a determined person. And you were her only child. She always had great ambitions for you."

"You knew this. You knew this about her and yet she was still your friend."

"Friends aren't people you particularly like for any special reason. You just like people because they're your friends."

"But if she was lying, then Eustace must have thought that I didn't want to see him again. All these years he's been thinking I simply let him down."

"But he wrote you a letter," said Alice.

"A *letter*?"

"Oh, Virginia, don't be so dense. That letter that came for you. The day before you went back to London." Virginia continued to stare blankly. "I know there was a letter. It came by the afternoon post, and it was on the table in the hall and I thought 'How nice' because you didn't get many letters. And then I went off to do something or other and when I came back the letter had gone. I presumed you'd taken it."

A letter. Virginia saw the letter. Imagined the envelope as white, the writing very black, addressed to her. Miss Virginia Parsons. Lying unattended and vulnerable upon that round table that still stood in the centre of the hall at Wheal House. She saw her mother come out of the drawing-room, perhaps on her way upstairs, pause to inspect the afternoon's mail. She was wearing the raspberry-red suit with the white silk shirt, and when she put out her hand to pick up the letter, her nails were painted the same raspberry-red, and her heavy gold charm bracelet made a jingling sound, like bells.

She saw her frown at the writing, the black masculine writing, inspect the postmark, hesitate for perhaps a second, and then slip the envelope into the pocket of her jacket and carry on with what she was doing, unperturbed, as though nothing had happened.

She said, "Alice, I never got that letter."

"But it was there!"

"Don't you see? Mother must have taken it. Destroyed it. She would, you know. She would say, 'It's all for Virginia's sake. For Virginia's own good.'"

Illusions were gone for ever, the veil torn away. She could look back with a cool, objective regard and see her mother the way she had really been, not merely snobbish and determined, but devious too. In some odd way, this was a relief. It had taken some effort, all these years, to sustain the legend of an irreproachable parent, even though

Virginia had been deceiving nobody but herself. Now, remembered, she seemed much more human.

Alice was looking upset, as though already regretting any mention of the letter.

"Perhaps it wasn't from Eustace."

"It was."

"How do you know?"

"Because if it had been from anyone else, then she would have given it back to me, with some excuse or other about opening it by mistake."

"But we don't know what was in the letter."

Virginia got off the table. "No. But I'm going to find out. Now. Will you stay here till the children wake up? Will you tell them I shan't be long?"

"But where are you going?"

"To see Eustace, of course," said Virginia, from the door.

"But you haven't drunk your coffee. I made you coffee and you haven't even drunk it. And what are you going to say to him? And how are you going to explain?"

But Virginia had already gone. Alice was speaking to an empty room, an open, swinging door. With an exclamation of exasperation, she put down her coffee cup and went to the door as though to call Virginia back, but Virginia was already out of earshot, running like a child through the tall summer grass, across the fields in the direction of Penfolda.

She took the field path because it would have taken too long to get into the car and turn it and drive back along the main road. And time was too precious to be wasted. They had already lost ten years, and there was not another moment to spare.

She was running, through a joyous morning of honey-scents and white daisies and tall grass that whipped at her bare legs. The sea was a dark, purplish blue, striped with ribbons of turquoise, and the horizon was blurred in a haze that promised great heat. She was running, long-legged, taking the steps of the stiles two at a time, and the ditches of the stubble fields brimmed with red poppies and the air was filled with the petals of yellow gorse flowers, blown to confusion, like confetti, by the sea-wind.

She came across the last field, and Penfolda lay ahead of her, the house and the long barns, and the little garden, wall-enclosed from the wind. She went over the last stile that led into the vegetable garden, and down the path and through the gate, and she saw that the cat and her half-Siamese kittens lay in the sun on the doorstep, and the front door stood open and she went indoors and called Eustace, and the house was dark after the brightness of the day outside.

"Who's that?"

It was Mrs. Thomas, carrying a duster, peering over the banister.

"It's me. Virginia. Virginia Keile. I'm looking for Eustace."

"He's just coming in from milking . . ."

"Oh, thank you." Without bothering to wait and explain, she went back out of doors, and started across the lawn, making for the cattle court and the milking parlour. But at that moment he appeared, coming through the gate that opened into the far side of the garden. He was in shirt sleeves, aproned, wearing rubber boots and carrying a polished aluminum pail of milk. Virginia stopped dead. He closed the latch of the gate behind him and looked up and saw her.

She had meant to be very sensible. To say, calmly and quietly, "I want to ask you about the letter you wrote me." But it didn't happen like that at all. For everything was said in that long moment, while they stood and looked at each other, and then Eustace set down his bucket and started towards her, and she ran down the slope of the grass and into his arms, and she was laughing, her face pressed into the front of his shirt, and he was saying, "It's all right. It's all right," just as though she were crying, not laughing. And Virginia said, "I love you," and then she burst into tears.

He said, "Of course I telephoned. Three or four times. But you were never there. It was always your mother and each time I felt more of a fool and each time she said that she'd tell you I'd called and that you'd ring me back. And I thought maybe you'd changed your mind. I thought perhaps you'd decided you had better things to do than come and have tea with someone like me and my old mother. I thought maybe your mother had talked you round. She didn't lose any love on me, not from the first moment she set eyes on me. But you knew that, didn't you?"

"Yes, I knew. And I wondered. Once, I nearly rang you up. I thought perhaps you'd forgotten . . . and then I lost my nerve. And then, out of the blue, my mother said we had to go back to London and after that, there wasn't any time. And in the train, I asked her, straight out, if you'd ever called and she said never. And I believed her. That was the terrible thing, I always believed her. I should have known. It was my fault, I should have known. Oh, Eustace, why was I such a ninny?"

They had come indoors, ostensibly to find a clean handkerchief for Virginia, and for no particular reason had stayed there, ending up, inevitably, in the kitchen, sitting at the scrubbed table, with the air filled with the smell of baking saffron bread, and the only sound to disturb them the slow ticking of the old-fashioned pendulum clock.

"You weren't a ninny," said Eustace. "You were seventeen. That was another of the things that bothered me. It would have been easy to persuade you, push you around, before you'd even had time to grow up and make up your own mind about things. That's what I said in the letter. When you never rang me back, I thought maybe you'd got cold feet. So I said that if you wanted to wait a couple of years, I'd be ready to wait too, see how we felt about things then." He grinned, ruefully. "It took some writing, I can tell you. I'd never said such things to a girl before, nor have since."

"And you thought I'd never even bothered to reply?"

"I didn't know what to think . . . And then, the next thing, I saw in the paper that you were getting married."

"Eustace, if I'd got the letter, I wouldn't have gone back to London. I'd have refused."

"You couldn't refuse, you were under age."

"I'd have had hysterics, then. A nervous breakdown. Made the most ghastly scenes. Made myself ill."

"You'd still have gone."

She knew that he was right. "But I'd have known you were there, waiting. And I would never have married Anthony. I would never have gone to Scotland. I would never have wasted all these years."

Eustace raised his eyebrows. "Wasted? They weren't wasted. What about Cara and Nicholas?"

Virginia's eyes stung with sudden tears. She said, "Now it's all too complicated."

He put his arms around her, kissed the tears away, pushed her hair back off her face. He said, "Things happen the way they're meant to. There's a pattern and a shape to everything. You look back and see it all. Nothing happens without a reason. Nothing is impossible, like meeting again, walking into The Mermaid's Arms and seeing you sitting there, just as though you'd never been away. Like a miracle."

"You didn't behave as though it were a miracle. In no time at all you were bawling at me."

"I was scared of getting hurt a second time. I was scared that I'd been mistaken about you, that all the things that were so important to your mother had become important to you, too."

"I told you. They were never important."

He took her hand in his. "After the picnic yesterday, I thought it was going to be all right. After being with you and Cara and Nicholas, and swimming and cooking the fish, and you all seeming to enjoy it so much, I thought then, coming up the cliff, that it was like being back where we started. And I thought I would be able to talk about that time, when you went back to London and I was left not knowing what had happened, and we never saw each other again. I thought we could have talked about it, perhaps made a new beginning."

"But I was thinking the same, you stupid man, and all you did was to tell me to go back to Scotland and learn how to be a farmer. I want to be farmer's wife, but I don't want to be a farmer. And I wouldn't know one end of an Aberdeen Angus herd from the other."

Eustace grinned again, faintly sheepish. "I told you, it was those photographs of Cara's. We'd seemed so close all day, and all at once I realized that we weren't close, we belonged to different worlds. We always have done, Virginia. A place like Kirkton and a little farm like Penfolda, well, you just don't talk about them in the same breath. And suddenly it seemed insane to imagine that I could ask you to leave all that, give it all up, just for the sake of being with me. Because that's all I've got to offer."

"And that's what I want. That's all I've ever wanted. Kirkton was Anthony's house. Without him to keep it going, it has no life at all. Anyway, I'm going to sell it. I decided last night. I shall have to go back, of course, break the news to everybody, put the whole thing in the lawyer's hands . . ."

"Have you thought about the children?"

"I never stop thinking about them. And they'll understand."

"It's their home."

"Penfolda's going to be their home." She smiled at the thought, and Eustace took her shoulders between his big hands and leaned forward to kiss her open, smiling mouth. "A new home and a new father," she finished when she had got her breath back.

But Eustace did not seem to be listening to her. "Talk of the devil," he said.

And Virginia heard the children, coming across the garden, talking, their voices high-pitched.

"Look, there are the kittens. Look, they're in the sun, and they haven't drunk their milk."

"Oh, leave them, Nicholas. They're having a sleep."

"This one isn't sleeping. It's got its eyes open. Look. Its eyes are open."

"I wonder where Mummy is? Mummy!"

"In here," called Eustace.

"Mummy, Aunt Alice Lingard wants to know if you're ever coming home again." Cara appeared at the kitchen door, her spectacles crooked, her hair hanging out of its slide. "She gave us some bacon and eggs, but we've been waiting and waiting and she says Mrs. Jilkes will think that she's been in a car accident, and died . . ."

"Yes," said Nicholas, appearing, hard on her heels, with a kitten spread-eagled by pin-like claws across the front of his sweater. "And we didn't wake up till ten past ten when Aunt Alice came up to see us, and we very nearly didn't have any breakfast at all, we very nearly just waited until lunch-time . . . but I was . . . so hungry . . ."

His voice trailed away. He had realized that nobody was talking but him. His mother and Eustace were simply sitting, watching him, and Cara was staring at her mother as though she had never seen her before. Nicholas was disconcerted. "Well, what's wrong? Why isn't anybody talking?"

"We're waiting for you to stop," said Virginia.

"Why?"

Virginia looked at Eustace. Eustace leaned forward to draw Cara towards him. Very gently, seriously, he set her spectacles straight. Then Nicholas saw that he was smiling.

"We've got something to tell you," said Eustace.

135